VOICE of
The Valley

SHEENA KOOPS

ORCA BOOK PUBLISHERS

"Big Yellow Taxi" copyright 1966-69 Siquomb Publishing Company.
Singer/songwriter: Joni Mitchell; Album: *Ladies of the Canyon*, May 1970.

Library and Archives Canada Cataloguing in Publication

Koops, Sheena, 1967-
Voice of the valley / Sheena Koops.

ISBN 1-55143-514-4

I. Title.

PS8621.O66V63 2006   jC813'.6   C2006-903099-5

First published in the United States, 2006
Library of Congress Control Number: 2006927981

Summary: A multi-layered coming-of-age story inspired by the
controversial flooding of Saskatchewan's Souris Valley.

Orca Book Publishers gratefully acknowledges the support for its publishing
programs provided by the following agencies: the Government of Canada through
the Book Publishing Industry Development Program and the Canada Council
for the Arts, and the Province of British Columbia through the
BC Arts Council and the Book Publishing Tax Credit.

Design and typesetting: Doug McCaffry
Cover illustration: Emily Carrington

Orca Book Publishers
PO Box 5626 Station B
Victoria, BC Canada
V8R 6S4

Orca Book Publishers
PO Box 468
Custer, WA USA
98240-0468

www.orcabook.com
www.sheenakoops.com
Printed and bound in Canada

09 08 07 06 • 6 5 4 3 2 1

Dedicated to my students:
past perfect, present perfect, future perfect;

Made possible by my parents:
Thanks for all the fish;

In memory of the valley:
Nenasnį ha.

There was great sorrow in the song and great joy, also,
that the privilege of sorrow had not yet been cast
from the people who sang it.

Jane Urquhart, Away

To Stacy

Tuesday, July 31

Dear Stacy,

Finally I have something interesting to tell you. No, I won't say, "I miss you sooo much. Sniff. Sniff." Or "Thinking of grade nine without you makes me sick." (Even though I do and it does!!!)

Ginger and I were in the valley yesterday. I know you get tired of me talking about the valley, but just listen to this one. I was wearing the Kaffiyeh. (Yes, that poor-excuse-for-a-tablecloth hula-hooped around my head.) I explored until sunset, mostly on foot. When it was time to leave, Ginger was a total pig. (It's like she knows I named her after my dead hamster and she wants to get even.) Onja's all lined up...she's ready to jump...okay, sidestep. Here she comes again...wait for it...now, bolt! You guessed it...I landed on my butt. Almost makes me want to ride with a saddle. *Almost.*

When I did get on, I rode up the winding trail and parked at Soldier Rock to wait for the stars. Big mistake. A flock of prairie chicken with wings beating like drummers flew from a patch of buck brush—right under Ginger. You know how cartoon characters run off cliffs? Ginger lunged sideways and I did the slow-motion fall. CRACK.

&%##%@??/** Did it ever hurt!

I was dizzy, but my eyes hooked onto this approaching shadow. I wasn't delirious…the shadow grew eyes and a face. And long black hair.

"Are you okay?" he said.

I nodded and tried to get up, but my head throbbed. I touched it. Wow, major goose egg! And shoot—I'd forgotten I was wearing the Kaffiyeh.

My head was roaring.

The shadow spoke again. "Let me help you." A soft voice, like grain spilling into a hopper. Shhhhhhhh.

He bent and took my hand. My teeth were chattering and his hand was so warm: I didn't want to let go.

I stood and got a better look: long hair and eyes like perfect skipping stones. "I hit my *rock* on the *head*," I said.

He laughed. I realized I'd done it again. Long live Mrs. Malaprop! Long live farm girls in *He*-gyptian *Ed*-dresses!

And then, just like I'd imagine in a Harlequin romance (you know I've only read one and that was because I was trapped in a one-book cabin during a four-day rain), he took off his jean jacket and held it open for me. I slipped into it and felt instantly warm. I'm sure I blushed. Then he asked, "If I help you onto your horse, do you think you can ride home?"

He walked toward Ginger, who was obviously concerned

about me as she ripped and tore at the grass. He made a kissing sound. My stomach flipped.

Sick, eh?

Anyway, Ginger let him catch her. He crouched and asked me to step on his back.

Weird. I think I laughed…my head was feeling a little better.

"We usually do it like this," I said, my voice all crackly. I demonstrated how to make a human stirrup with my hands meshed together. He smiled—an *amazing* smile—like the moment the sun rests on the horizon, then leaves the world in a trance of orange, yellow and red. (How's *that* for mushy…maybe writing Harlequin romances is in my future!) He wove his hands together. I stepped and he threw me. I had to grab Ginger's neck or I'd have flown off the other side!

At the Texas gate, he was going to lead us right over the steel poles. I explained how to open the wire fence. Of course it would have been easier to get down and do it myself, but I was too busy staring at him. My arms inside his jean jacket felt tingly and achy. (Yep, I felt like a character in a Harlequin romance.) And the goose egg? Forgot it.

We didn't talk as he led us home. It was totally unreal.

Finally, at the end of my lane, he said, "Okay, see you around," and retraced his steps. I didn't say anything, but I watched him until I couldn't tell him from the dark blue of night.

I went straight to the house and sat down in the big ivory chair, horse pants and all. Good thing Mom and Dad were in town celebrating or she'd have kicked me out of the chair, goose egg and all.

I'm not sure how long I sat there before I heard the truck pull up. Then I remembered…I was still wearing the Kaffiyeh and this guy's jean jacket. I ran for cover.

You must be ready to puke. I know we hate boy-crazy girls, but this is different. Isn't it? Do you think I'm losing it? Please tell me if I'm being too strange. I wouldn't talk like this to anyone—except you.

I really missed you at camp this year. As usual, no one could get my name right. The director read off her clipboard: ON *JJJ*A! I went to her afterward and said, "My name is On Ya, as in 'that shirt looks good *on ya*.'" She said, "Okay, On—JJJJa." The cook called me Tonya at every meal. My counselor called me Sonia for the first week. Finally I told her the whole story of how Mom met the Russian Anja (with an *A*) in Egypt and how they became lifelong pen pals and promised to name their first daughters after one another. She said, "So your name is spelled wrong, but pronounced right." I said, "You've got it."

Camp was…okay, but most girls our age are pathetic. Really, how many hours can they stand in front of a mirror? Boring!

Speaking of boring. This summer is going to be a killer. Nothing ever happens. I'll probably prowl around the valley a lot. Looking for trouble. Ha.

Your new friends Amber and Cayley sound like fun. Are they really into fencing? The only kind of fencing I've done is with barbed wire and posts. Ha.

Thanks for listening, Stace. I hope I'm not too weird.

Your best friend,

Onja

P.S. I wonder how the guy with long hair is. He's taller than me, probably 5´10˝, with a strong, thin face. I'm guessing he's in grade ten, or maybe eleven. Wish I had a picture to show you.

P.P.S. I'll be fifteen, two weeks from yesterday. 365 + 13 = 378 days to my license! Can't wait to drive to Medicine Hat to see you! (Dream, dream, dream.)

Above Her Valley

The bridge, with its chalky stone double arches, was the first landmark to catch her eyes. The chestnut mare's pace was a slowing metronome as hooves beat gravel. Onja held the leather reins taut in her right hand. "Whoa, girl." They stopped on the hill above the valley. Her valley. Her eyes swept east and west, tidying the images: a flock of pelicans landing on the narrow river, a far border of cattails that grew thicker into a hay slough, a skinny poled fence with sagging barbed wire keeping everything neither in nor out.

A long black car glinted by the artesian well near the valley's opposite wall, fins fishtailing like exhaust. Must be someone from the other side, Onja thought.

Ginger stamped her front hoof and shook. Like a drenched dog, Onja observed. She grabbed the coarse copper mane and managed to keep her balance. "Easy, girl," she said, placing her hand on the mare's glistening shoulder. The energy of twitching muscle, surging blood and beating sun jolted through her arm to her heart. She'd been ten when her father had brought home the three-year-old filly. Onja had overheard her mother: "Wayne, that prancing Arab is too much horse for her." Her dad had answered, "The mare's only half Arabian, and Onja has a good seat. She can handle it."

Onja clenched her teeth. How did he know I had a good seat? she thought. The only horse advice he'd given was after watching me fall off my Shetland pony.

He'd yelled, "Why don't you roll?"

Wish I'd yelled back, "Because I don't practice falling off." Instead, I just lay there in the dirt, trying to catch my wind.

The early days graduating to Ginger had been tense: one bare foot stepped on, two out-of-control gallops, three refusals to be caught...but in the last four years they'd worked out the kinks in the partnership. And Onja had learned to read equine signals. Ears back: fear. Ears forward: curiosity. Head bunting: impatience. Foot stomping: more impatience.

The sun blinked. "Shade...we need shade," Onja said, nudging the horse and snapping softly with her tongue.

Her eyes fixed on the mountainous erratic beside the bridge. Onja's mother had explained that the word erratic came from the Latin word *erraticus* meaning "wandering." Onja thought of these boulders, like Soldier Rock, at the other border of her valley, abandoned on the prairie like baby mammoths by the retreating ice. A lick of breeze teased through her hair. She relaxed into the downward gait. The shade of the bridge grew with each grind of Ginger's hooves.

The erratic below, with its smooth top and spool-like sides, was separated from the riverbed by a wide ring of

pulverized earth. She imagined an ancient buffalo herd—
before roads, fences and the bridge—with no shade for
miles, mingling, darkening the valley under a pulsating
sun. She could see them clustered around the erratic, each
bunting their way to the inner circle to scratch their thick
hides on the rubbing stone.

A flash of black disappeared, drawing Onja's eyes to the
smooth and sloping coulees on the other side, a crazy quilt
of sun-washed dun, gold and sage tossed onto a hastily
made bed.

Onja yawned and stretched her sleeping spine. The
first day of August, she thought, and exactly one month
since Stacy'd left for Medicine Hat. What's Alberta got that
Saskatchewan doesn't? Maybe more oil and coal and cows,
but I'd be so homesick if I was Stacy—even two weeks of
camp was too much for me—yet Stacy seems to be having
the time of her life.

A killdeer screeched its name twice. A distant cow bel-
lowed in the community pasture and was soon answered by
her kind. The calls drifted into Onja's inner soundscape like
twilight coyotes singing of wolf cousins or flatland trains
dreaming of mountains. Audible and unnoticed.

Muktuk barked and gave a zigzag chase after a blur of
brown on the other side of the river.

"Muuuck Tuuuck." Onja elongated the vowels like a chant,
her voice dry and empty against the two miles of valley
floor. She listened to the silence left by her call. Muktuk, she
thought. I wonder if those words have ever, in the history of

humankind, been shouted in this valley. "Muktuk," she whispered, tasting the heat.

Then: an almost human scream. Onja shuddered. Crap, she thought, he got it. The black Lab trotted from the ditch just across the bridge with a limp rabbit dangling from his mouth. Why can't he just eat dog food?

I hate senseless death, she thought. Like when Dad brings home deer, necks limp, tongues hanging out. Or prairie chicken, cold like feather pillows. Even when they butchered chicken, Onja hid in the house and then refused to eat anything they'd processed themselves. They had names, she thought. How could I eat Freckles?

The dog reached the double arching bridge and turned west into the riverbed when Onja was halfway down the hill. He'd joined the family eight years ago, bringing his own name, which meant whale blubber in Inuit, and a ring of white hair around his neck. Her dad had said the six-month-old puppy had rarely been let off his rope. Maybe we should have called him Hunter, or Gunner, like Grandpa Tom's old Lab, Onja thought.

Her eyes followed him along the narrow, meandering river until he disappeared behind a coulee wall where the fence led to the river and separated the community pasture from Stacy's father's pasture. Onja mentally jogged along with Muktuk, her thoughts bouncing. Was it just two nights ago she'd met the young man with the eyes as black as summer fallow?

Ginger's hooves displaced dust and stones. She wondered where Longhair was *right now* as she rode onto the valley flat.

Near the chalky bridge, Onja swung her right leg over Ginger's head, riding sidesaddle for a few plodding moments. Onja's sweaty thighs cooled slightly in the gentle wind. She closed her eyes and breathed the August perfume of foamy horsehide, swathed clover and riverbed reeds. *If only I could memorize this smell,* she mused. *Recall it in the middle of a blizzard. Savor it on a long car ride.* The sun's lashes brushed her face, and she rolled her head to one side and then the other under its smile. *I wonder if Longhair's thinking of me?*

Ginger dug her hooves in and Onja lunged for the mare's coarse mane to keep from falling backward. Blood-red paint screamed *Save the Valley* up and down the closest cement arch. Ginger's muscles tensed and she sidestepped, her head pulling at the reins.

"Easy, girl, whoa," Onja cooed.

Horse and girl were motionless, considering the graffiti. *Save the Valley? From what?* she wondered.

Onja jumped from her mount and landed on both feet. *Just like an Indian in an Old West movie,* she mused. *Too bad there was no one around to see it.*

She adjusted the pack straps on her own shoulders, knotted the reins and led Ginger onto the bridge. The mare snorted, eyes on the glaring color, ears twisting forward then back.

"Take it easy, girl," Onja soothed, "it's just a bit of paint."

Ginger veered sharply to the right when her back hooves clipped onto the wooden boards. With a little prancing and trot they passed the red-letter message and left the bridge in peace.

The ditch grass, cropped short by recent swathing, poked through Onja's socks. Speargrass, appropriately named, she thought as it stabbed her ankles. She stepped over the wide bed of drying wild grasses. Ginger stopped and lowered her head to nuzzle the future hay. "None of that," Onja scolded, tightening her lead. The mare followed, but kicked the swath with each hoof. A pixie dust of faded purple and yellow clover, pale gray sage, honey-colored wild oats and sweetgrass puffed into the breeze, following them down the dirt riverbed and onto the rocky edge of the river.

Onja loosely looped the reins around Ginger's neck. The mare began to graze on the evergreen grasses at the edge of the river. A grove of cattails and reeds met Onja as she stepped into the coolness beside the bridge.

This was their routine.

She squatted and swished her hands in the water like a raccoon, the memory of an Ice Age delicious on her skin. She patted her face; the droplets quickly air-dried in the midday heat.

In the darkness beneath her bridge, one foot on a round stone, the other on an oiled timber plank, she listened. The world was alive with sound: whirr of dragonfly, flute song of meadowlark, gurgle of water.

Her stomach rumbled and she took her lunch from the pack: a Mason jar of orange juice, a ham sandwich on pita bread, and a McIntosh apple. She set the lunch on a concrete slab and took a deep breath, evaluating the perfection of her dining room. Ginger nickered as if to say, what about me? Onja tossed her a carrot—garden dirt clinging to the cracks—and sat down with her back against a bridge post.

A splash. Onja looked under the bridge across the water. Circles rippled into view behind the erratic. A little perch? she wondered.

Her eyes followed the growing rings, then leapt to the boulder. Last spring she and Stacy had fished from the flat top of the erratic. Onja reached for a handful of stones and side-armed them at the rock.

Stacy. It had all started in school. Elbow deep in the kindergarten sandbox, they'd promised to be best friends forever.

Onja glared at the lazy river full of chaotic rings caused by the stones bouncing off the boulder; the water seemed deeper and darker.

Fishing was the only thing Stacy considered fun in the valley and the only killing Onja didn't classify as murder. They'd caught jackfish one afternoon and kept them in a five-gallon pail of river water. Later that day, in the Claibourn's kitchen, they'd helped Onja's brother, Thomas, scale, clean, batter and fry the fish. What a feast! Then Onja swallowed a bone. Her dad told her to eat a piece of bread to catch the thin white needle.

That day was the last time they'd hung out under the bridge. That was before they knew Stacy was moving. Everything had happened at a galloping speed.

"Ouch." Another needle of speargrass bit her ankle. She reached forward and plucked the invader from her sock.

A cattail reed swayed into her shoulder. She snapped it off at the head. The dense brown fur fluffed beneath her burrowing fingernails, multiplying in size like popcorn.

Onja wondered what her best friend was doing in Medicine Hat at that very moment. She seemed so far away from Palliser, Saskatchewan: population 119, including cats and dogs. Why did things have to change and get so screwed up?

She dug for a notepad and pen in her pack. She dated the top of the page and wrote, "Dear…"

A rustle in the reeds interrupted her. A beaver? Onja wondered. A skunk? She stood, ready to inch forward or back.

Beneath Her Bridge

Ginger nickered.

"Do you need a *reservation* to get into this place?"

Longhair.

Onja squinted through her darkness, seeing only his outline against the light.

He stepped across her stones and under her bridge, stooping to protect his head. "I can show you my reservation card." He pulled a can of Coke out of his satchel. "You know all the spots around here, eh?"

Onja swallowed. The bridge seemed to close in around them, changing from an open and empty restaurant to a covered booth.

"How many cat's tails have you murdered today?" His voice fell between spoken word and song.

Onja looked at her feet. A line of white puffy cattail seed trailed to the water. Who is this guy? She smirked, then sat against the post; she didn't know what else to do. He sat right beside her, arm against arm, before he settled into his own space.

She smelled laundry soap and sweat. It was a good smell. She inhaled again, slowly. If I could bottle it, she thought, I'd hide it in the back of my closet inside my note jar. I wonder what he keeps in his closet. Her cheeks burned as if the bridge had opened up and the sun was laughing directly on her face. She clutched her notebook.

He raised the Coke to his mouth, drank, then licked his lips. "Want some?"

Onja coughed. "Uh…no thanks. I've got some orange juice."

They listened to the rushes swishing like taffeta on nylon.

His left leg was an inch away from her right, his other knee tucked to his chest with his arm slung across. Her back was straight. He sat slightly hunched. Her hands were meshed over her notebook. His hand, nearest hers, pulled at a fray on his jean cuff. He adjusted his seat, his thigh against hers. A whistle was growing like a headache inside her skull.

The river trickled so slowly it sounded like coins tossed into a wishing well, she thought—plunk, plink, plunk.

"What kind of music do you like?" he asked.

Your voice for starters, she thought. "Country," she said, "and other stuff." She and Stacy loved jumping on the bed playing badminton guitars to Mom's ABBA records. "Super Trouper." "Money, Money, Money." "Rock Me." "Does Your Mother Know?" She didn't dare admit it.

"Do you like 'Daddy's Girl'?"

"Pardon me?"

"You know," he said and then began to sing in a mocking, overly accentuated twang, "Daddy's Girl, Daddy's Girl, she's the center of Daddy's world…"

Goose bumps nipped at her arms.

"I know I'm Daddy's number one 'cause he loves me like I was his son…"

She laughed. "What was that?"

"What? You don't like the lyrics?" He ribbed Onja with his elbow.

She lunged away from the newness of his touch. "Are you kidding? Those are the stupidest words I've ever heard."

He laughed. "Yeah, Mom hates them too. Must be a girl thing. I think they're kinda sweet."

Onja held her body rigid. The playful conflict kept her attuned to his body, like a negative magnet beside a positive. She could feel the wall of energy.

Onja heard the rumble of a nearing vehicle on gravel. She laughed nervously and sent herself back to the bridge post.

"So, what kind of music do I like?" His voice was a joke before the punch line. "Well…" He pretended his thumb was a microphone. "I like a little of everything. Classic Canadian rock when I'm driving…"

"You have your license?" Don't look at him, she willed herself. Don't gawk. Don't even say another word. Your voice sounds like a grade three student's.

"Of course! I don't always walk all the way down here. Now…where was I?"

The black car. It was his?

"…R and B when I'm relaxing. Hip-hop for working, Athabaska fiddling for jigging…"

A horn blasted. The bridge shook and silver dust poured onto their hair and shoulders as a heavy truck passed overhead. Onja scrambled to cover her untouched lunch.

They listened as the vehicle lumbered away. The young man looked at the notebook now lying on her lap and leaned toward it.

"Dear…who? Do you have a boyfriend?" He took another drink, swallowed, then stood. He crushed the can sideways with his hands, folded it into his pocket and sat down.

Onja felt like she was floating. "Um. Yes…at camp…last week…he's nice…Victor. His name is…Victor." Get real! she thought. *Nice*? And did I really say his name is Victor?

Her heart was tight. She could feel every pulse. What now? She took a deep breath. *Keep your head.* She looked at the dark-eyed stranger, daring and fearing him to catch her in the lie.

He was now sitting cross-legged. He took another Coke from his satchel and turned to study Onja.

Does he actually believe me? she wondered. Isn't it kind of obvious that no guy would ever be interested in me?

Onja took out her pita bread as she evoked her mental scorecard. Stacy: curly blond hair; Onja: straight, straw hair; Stacy: killer smile; Onja: half-baked smile; Stacy: chocolate brown eyes; Onja: blue slough eyes; Stacy: hourglass; Onja: spaghetti strings.

Guys liked girls like Stacy, and Onja didn't blame them. Her best friend was cute and fun. Onja was shy and average, except her eyes. When she wore her dusty blue bathrobe, her eyes were almost pretty in the dresser mirror. Big deal, she thought. Who except family saw her in her bathrobe? Sometimes when she brushed her hair a hundred strokes, it was as shiny as foxtail. And once, when she'd just finished a big laugh with her brother, she caught her reflection in the window and it twinkled back from the night.

One afternoon when she had tried on a really expensive pair of jeans at The Gap, in Regina, she actually didn't look that bad, but of course, no one was around to see. Same old, same old, she thought. And her mother didn't buy them for her.

Longhair interrupted Onja's scorekeeping. "I have a girlfriend up north."

The butterflies landed; she knew this feeling. She'd had it when she read her first letter from Stacy, with all her new places, new friends, and here it was again, stalking her right into the valley.

My life makes no sense, she thought, pulling her foot across her knee. She dug in her sock, purging the freeloading burrs. I am sitting under a bridge with an incredibly hot guy, he even carries a satchel, and I don't even know his name, but already I'm jealous of his girlfriend. She reached behind her shoulder and snapped another cattail.

"Murderer."

His smile is like vanilla ice cream, she thought, smiling, with rainbow sprinkles on top.

"How's your head?"

Her hand touched the tender bump. "It's okay." She paused. "I guess I should say thank you for the help." She sneaked a quick look at his face. He looked different today. His hair, she thought, it's in a ponytail. It makes his jaw seem stronger; he looks older. And his eyes are ageless, like a pharaoh's.

He shrugged. "It was no problem."

"No problem, yeah right. You just about walked me all the way home. It must have been an inconvenience, at the least."

A smile leapt across his face. "What were you wearing on your head?"

Onja glanced at him peripherally. He wasn't laughing. "It's a Kaffiyeh. I pronounce it Keh—fear—eee, but I don't know if that's right. My mom brought it home from Egypt."

"Egypt?"

"When she graduated from university, before she married Dad, her parents took her on a tour of the Holy Land…you should see our living room. Mom collects camels. She says she started with the wooden camels carved by craftsmen in Egypt, but now she has ceramic, glass, iron, papier-mâché…at least it's easy buying her Christmas presents."

"How do you pronounce that head thing again?"

"Keh—fear—eee."

"It looked incredible when you were running your horse," he said, taking a yellow apple from his artist bag. "Sort of Batman meets Lawrence of Arabia."

She smiled. He was the first person other than her family or Stacy who had seen her parade in the Kaffiyeh. She tried to neutralize her grin by concentrating on the ancient erratic, but the delight remained on her face. "Thanks, I guess."

He took a bite of his apple. She crunched into hers. They sat together and crackled and slurped the juicy fruit. He took another drink. She untwisted the lid of the Mason jar and held the jar to her thin lips. She caught a dribble of orange juice with the back of her hand as it rolled down her chin. Both were quiet for a long time.

Onja spoke, surprising herself. "What were *you* doing in the valley?"

"You mean, when I wasn't watching you?" He grinned. "Just kidding. I was helping my mom at an archaeology dig not far from there." He looked up the river where Muktuk had loped with the rabbit.

"Archaeology?"

"Yes. You know. People looking for the past."

"I know what archaeology is," Onja said, the smile still pulling at her mouth, "but are you saying there's archaeology in *my* valley."

"There's a small dig this side of the big *head* where you hit your *rock*." Her inside-out grin returned, remembering her first words to him. But what was he talking about? Archaeology?

He nodded downstream. "There's a major dig about a mile that way."

"Since when?" A thought more felt than articulated edged Onja's consciousness: nothing happens in my valley without my knowledge of it.

"I don't know, but Mom's been helping out for a couple of weeks."

"But why? Are they looking for a Saskatchewan Sphinx or something?"

"Mom says it's research. Says the government will feel less guilty if they have some artifacts and reports." He looked down.

"Wait a minute. You're joking, right?" She pulled a stray lock of hair off her eyes.

"No, I'm not joking. Are you?" He leaned forward and crooked his neck, face toward hers.

"Joking about what?" She pulled her head slightly back.

"About not knowing." He leaned even closer, examining her face.

"Not knowing what?" She looked down his face from his eyes to his lips and then quickly over his shoulder.

"They're planning to flood this valley."

A cold quiver ran back down her neck and into her spine. Onja had often heard rumors about building a dam that would flood the valley, but it was always talk, wasn't it?

She swallowed. "Do you really think they could flood this valley? Look how narrow the river is here, and over at Stony Crossing—that's where I was riding when we met—it's always dry by this time of year. Where would they get the water from?"

He shrugged. "I could take you to the dig site."

"Sure, I'd like that," Onja answered before thinking.

She'd always loved the idea of archaeology, but it happened in places like Egypt. She'd been an Egypt freak ever since grade six, when her mom had taken her to the University of Regina for a marathon of King Tut and other Egyptian documentaries. She'd dreamed of archaeology, but not in her valley. Not so close to home. It just wasn't…right.

"How about tomorrow?" he added, standing up. He stepped onto a stone the size and shape of a curling rock and waved his arms back and forth, like a tightrope walker.

"Sure," she said, her soft voice disguising her enthusiasm.

"There's this real radical guy, Jones. He's like the original conspiracy theory guy. Has some theories about this valley too. I could introduce you."

"Sure, but…how will I get there?"

"Etthen Mercredi at your service, oh Lady of the Flying Keh—fear—ee." He leapt forward, bowed and took her hand. "I can pick you up." He stretched lower and kissed her knuckles.

Onja hesitated, then screeched and yanked her hand from his. He froze, pucker still on his lips. Their eyes locked, and she forgot Stacy, forgot the valley, forgot real girlfriends or imagined boyfriends. She was just a girl with a guy beneath a bridge, and that was good enough. And then she laughed, from deep inside her belly.

Etthen looked like he'd had the wind knocked out of him. A slow smirk dawned on his face. "Guess I won't try that again."

She took several deep breaths and her nervous laughter subsided. "No, I bet you won't." I must be glowing like I've just torn through the finish line in a race, she thought. She thrust her hand forward. "EEE Than. Is that how you say your name?"

"Eh THAN," he said, emphasizing the second syllable as he took her hand to help her up.

"Eh THAN, my name is Onja." She also emphasized the last syllable—YA, adding, "O—N—J, as in Jack—A...I live on a farm...oh yeah...you know where I live."

"Pleased to meet you, Onja," he said, still shaking her hand.

She opened her mouth as if to speak. His hand was loose in hers. *He said my name right.*

"What's your last name?" he asked, then jumped to another stone.

"Claibourn, Onja Claibourn."

"Any relation to Bond, James Bond?"

A now-familiar warmth rubbed her cheeks. He got her again!

"You're funny, Claibourn, Onja Claibourn."

He pirouetted on the stone, then jolted away from her, runners splashing in the water.

Showing off, she thought. Her chest burned.

He stopped and patted Ginger. "My mom and I are renting that farm over there." He nodded toward the old road carved into the side of the hill. Onja knew it wound side to side so that the horses could pull the carts in or out of the valley during the pioneer days. It was little more than a cow trail now, leading to Stacy's farm. *Stacy's* farm?

Her eyes widened.

"So, I'll phone you. You're in the book, right?" Etthen's voice trailed down to her as he climbed the side of the bank.

"Under Wayne," Onja called back.

The mare watched him as he left Onja alone in the coolness of her bridge. Ginger turned to her girl and nickered like a sympathetic mother: *There, there, dear.*

Onja stared at the cattails until their shape blurred into another image. Etthen's square jaw; lips tight and in control. His eyes were caves of mischief—inviting and startling, as if bats might fly out at any minute. He wore his jeans as if they were the most comfortable clothes in the world. He was tall and thin, and when he leaned into her arm, he felt solid as rock. When she had first seen him, she hadn't guessed how amazing he was under his jean jacket. *Jean* jacket? Shoot! She'd forgotten to return it. At least now she knew his name. And where he lived. "Eh THAN," she whispered, punching the last syllable like someone learning a new language.

At Home

Wayne Claibourn, Onja's father, was stacking steaming dishes higher and higher into the blue dish rack. He's like a machine, Onja thought. Nobody can help him because any other hand would scald off from the boiling rinse water.

Onja's mother, Sylvia Reid-Claibourn, was making egg foo yong and chicken stir-fry. She had taken a Chinese cooking class with some of her friends from the University Women's Club. Onja was glad the women's group was interested in more than books; her mother was becoming an awesome cook.

My teeth are watering, Onja thought, smelling the sautéing onion and chicken. An Icelandic seaman on a TV documentary about whaling introduced this saying to the family. His teeth watered when he thought about eating whale blubber. Whale blubber? Onja had never made the connection before. Muktuk's name meant whale blubber in Inuit. Onja wondered how to say "whale blubber" in Icelandic.

She took five plates down from the cupboard before remembering that Thomas wasn't home anymore. First Stacy moved, then Thomas. He had sent a postcard from Lethbridge: a metal wolf sculpture at the university campus.

Wrote that he was "Having a blast."

Alberta again. What's so blame great about the province next door that everybody had to move there? I'll never live in Alberta, Onja promised herself. They're a bunch of rednecks, at least that's what her auntie claimed. Auntie Rose wore scrunchy, flowing skirts and floppy hats. Dad called her a flower child.

Onja looked at her father, busy at the sink. His neck was burnt copper. His cap protected his bald head and tanned face, but left his neck open to the sun's attack. Was he a redneck too? The fifth plate clattered as she returned it to the cupboard.

Sylvia called "Supper" over the banister to get Leigh's attention. As her younger sister skipped up the stairs, Onja wondered what weird ten-year-old drama she'd been enacting. She just didn't *get* Leigh. How could she be so happy, all day long, by herself? She just played and played and never needed any friends. It wasn't that she didn't *have* friends—she had plenty—but she rarely asked any of them to the farm. Onja kind of envied that a person could be her own best friend, though she'd never admit this to Leigh.

The Claibourn family, minus Thomas, sat on tall stools at the island table in the middle of the kitchen. They held hands and bowed their heads. Leigh led a family blessing and the rest joined in:

> *Thank you for the world so sweet.*
> *Thank you for the food we eat.*
> *Thank you for the birds that sing.*
> *Thank you, God, for everything.*
> *In Jesus' name, Amen.*

Onja squeezed Leigh and Sylvia's hands. They squeezed back. She raised her head and looked into her dad's blue eyes. What was he smirking about?

Her mother asked, "So, what were you doing all day?"

Onja lifted her eyes to the window. "I…I was just hanging out in the valley."

"At Stony Crossing?"

"The bridge." Onja grabbed the plate of soy sauce omelettes. It felt heavy in her hands.

"Doing what?" Wayne raised his caterpillar eyebrows.

"Just hanging out…with Ginger." Onja served herself. She'd been replaying the afternoon over and over, but there was no flipping way her family was getting any of the details.

"Nobody else?" Sylvia asked. Her voice was half baby talk, half interrogator, Onja thought.

"Why?" Onja paused with a bite halfway to her mouth. She looked at her mother.

"No reason. I was just wondering if you'd met anyone new lately."

Onja realized that no one else seemed interested in the food; they were all smiling like cats with a secret. Leigh's head was bent slightly forward, her eyes shooting intrigue behind strawberry bangs. Her mother's neck was twisted sideways like a two-dimensional hieroglyphic. Her short black hair framed black eyes, black eyebrows and a taupe complexion. Her dad's mouth was slightly open in a stalled laugh.

"Actually, I did meet someone new," she said, casually slipping her fork into her mouth. She swallowed and choked on the last bit of food. "Etthen Mercredi…he's living at Stacy's farm."

"He's been there for two weeks," Leigh piped in. "They came the day after you left for camp. He's so HOT!"

Onja coughed and grabbed for water.

"Leigh." Wayne's voice was stern.

"Oh yeah, I forgot," Leigh continued. "I have to talk old-fogey language when you're around. He's very handsome, Father."

How does she get away with talking to Dad like that? Onja stewed. If I'd said something like that…

"What do you know about handsome, little girl?" Sylvia asked and then winked at Onja.

Onja smiled, trying to be the all-knowing big sister, but with Etthen's name fresh on her tongue she was afraid she'd give herself away. She took a helping of stir-fry.

Her mother continued, "I met Celine—that's Etthen's mother—and Etthen yesterday in town while I was getting the mail. She's an archaeologist. That woman has the most gorgeous, long black hair."

Like Etthen, Onja thought.

"A real archaeologist next door," Sylvia continued. "I hope she comes to visit us at the museum after I'm back from holidays."

I wonder if she's been to Egypt and done real archaeology, Onja thought. She imagined Celine Mercredi in the Valley of the Kings, Queen Nefertiti driving her chariot across her tomb to the next world.

"Do you think *Etthen* has a *story*?" Leigh said, leaning even closer into the family.

You're not saying his name right, Onja thought.

"He might be running from the law. Hiding out in the hills. Alan Kutarna says that Jesse James held up at his great-great-grandmother's house in Palliser for two nights, then went back to North Dakota."

Why is Dad still looking at me? Onja pushed a thinly sliced carrot off her plate.

"How romantic." Leigh sighed. "An outlaw next door." She batted her eyes like a southern belle.

"Well, he's taking me to see an archaeology dig tomorrow," Onja announced sharply. Her tone mellowed. "Dad, is it true that there are plans to flood the valley?"

Wayne looked out the north window and paused for a few moments before speaking. "There've been plans to build a dam in these parts since the thirties. When Palliser explored this area of Saskatchewan, he called it a desert, and sometimes it *is* a desert, not enough rain to drown an ant. That's why they talk about a dam. But it has been mostly talk until now. This time I think it's going to happen. There's a lot of activity in the valley."

Onja's heart tightened into a fist. That's *my* valley he's talking about. My bridge, my pump house, my swimming hole, my Stony Crossing. How could they flood *my* valley? It would be like flooding someone's backyard…swings, sandbox, tree house, garden.

The backdrops of childhood, gone.

"But Dad—" Onja wrinkled her forehead. Don't panic. Think. That valley is dry. We almost live in a desert. Palliser was mostly right. She smiled, relieved by her reasoning. "There's not enough water, right?"

"That's the question. Some say it would take forty years for the runoff to fill a dam. The government says twenty. Your great-uncle West says five."

"What do you mean, 'the government says'? How serious is this?" Onja straightened her back and pushed her hands against the island, shooting her tall chair back.

"Like I said, this time they mean business. West has sold all his valley land, and just look at the archaeology. They must be spending tons of money paying those crews. Money talks."

"It can't be about money." Onja spoke with authority.

Her father rested both elbows on the table and leaned toward his daughter. "Everything is about money."

Onja stared at her dad. The armor of disbelief held her body rigid.

"Leigh, help me clear the table," Sylvia interrupted. She piled the dishes, utensils on top, and handed them to Leigh. Sylvia reached for Onja's milk-filmed glass. Clinking and clicking filled the room.

"Who wants dessert?" Sylvia tempted from the counter.

Onja left the table. The rest of the family stared; pineapple upside-down cake was her favorite.

Onja lay in bed until the moon flooded her room. What would a dam look like? Would it be cement? Rocks?

Wood? The little swimming hole by Stony Crossing had a small dam made of wood. Stop the stupid talk, she barked at herself. There's not going to be a damn dam! There's no water. She breathed deeply; a weight—that she hadn't realized lay on her chest—lifted.

She looked up at the cherished poster of Superman pinned to her ceiling.

Tomorrow she would see Etthen again. *I can't believe I told him I had a boyfriend. What got into me?*

Superman, with his denim blue eyes, was her measure of perfection, but brown eyes were starting to have their own appeal.

\

From the Farm

Onja heard the familiar rap on her door. KNOCK, knock, knock, KNOCK, KNOCK, pause, KNOCK, KNOCK. It was the pattern Grandpa used to punch on his horn as he drove up the lane: Shave and a haircut—two bits.

She moaned and rolled over in bed to see the clock. "Dad, it's only six fifty-five. Give me a break."

"Thought you'd like to know that your ride to the valley will be here soon." Her father's voice was almost playful.

Onja threw the covers off and sat up straight. "Hurray!" she cried sarcastically, attempting to hide her true delight.

She stumbled to the mirror. Her hair looked right out of the eighties: big and out of control. If I wet it, she thought, it won't dry before he gets here. She pulled a brush through the tangles. "Ouch." She gathered a handful and tore at the knots, eyes fixed on her reflection. "Great, now it just looks oily!"

Onja dug in her top drawer. Rainbow elastics, a horse-shoe, a letter from a pen pal in Egypt, an old hotel room key, postcards from Scotland and Estonia, a bandana. What a wonderful mess, she thought. She flipped her slick mop upside down and tied the bandana at the nape of her neck.

She looked back into the mirror and tried to smile. "Sweet," she said, frowning.

Any other morning, Onja would have left the mirror with that frown on her mind. This morning, she maintained eye contact. She willed a shy smile into her reflection. Then a blooming smile. Next a laugh smile. She stood up straight and smiled with confidence. Is this what the early morning girls at camp do in the bathroom for an hour? Onja wondered.

She looked out her basement bedroom window over the tall, dry grass. The sky was cloudless. She remembered another morning, when she was about eight or nine, and her dad woke her up at 5:00 AM. He needed help starting the tractor. Thomas must have been at hockey camp or something, she thought. She and her father drove past the pig barn and corral, and just beyond a lake of blue washed into view. Flax in bloom.

She dressed quickly in a tank top and cut-off jeans, then slapped coconut sunscreen on her legs, arms, neck and face. Her slippery fingers opened her closet door. Won't need a coat, she thought, even as Etthen's jean jacket caught her eye. She slipped it off the hanger and pressed the denim into her face. A musky clean smell sent chills down to her bare toes. Better give it back, she thought.

She ran up the stairs, two at a time, and into the kitchen where half a pot of porridge was bubbling on the stove. She dug in.

Her father strolled into the kitchen, poured himself a cup of coffee and sat across from her. "I wish I was coming with you."

Onja looked up from her porridge and lowered her brows. "Why?"

His eyes were child blue for a moment. "I dig in the dirt for a living. So do the archaeologists. I guess I've always had a professional interest."

She scooped a spoonful of porridge and thought of her mother's photo album. Sylvia wore a mesh hat and red jeans as she rode her camel toward the sandy pyramids at Giza. Onja took another mouthful and said in a mushy voice, "I doubt they'd find much that's interesting around here."

"I wouldn't be so certain about that." Wayne gulped a drink of coffee. "Saskatchewan has an interesting history, just like every other place on the planet, but much of it is unrecorded. That makes archaeology *here* even more mysterious, don't you think?"

Onja shrugged and raised her eyebrows as if to say, *Whatever.*

She grasped the bowl with both hands, as her dad had taught her to when she was little, and slurped the last bit of milk. She looked over Wayne's shoulder at the kitchen clock, took a deep breath and got up for some orange juice, then sat again with her father, neither of them speaking. She circled the rim of her glass with her finger, trying to get it to sing, then wandered over to the living room window. Nothing.

She watched the living room clock: Tick tock. One Mississauga. Two Mississauga. Three Mississauga. The clock—a birthday gift from Sylvia to Wayne—was made in the art form intarsia, a wooden puzzle. Oak for a prairie elevator, rolling hills in cherry and beech, and white pine for the moon. Each hour had a sample of a prairie crop seed displayed behind glass. One was oats; two, flax; three, barley; four, peas; five, sunflower; six, durum; seven, lentils; eight, canary; nine, canola; ten, rye; eleven, mustard; and twelve, wheat.

It was half past lentils.

The door slammed. "Hello," Onja called. No answer. Dad must have gone outside, she thought. She bounded to the bay window just as the tractor chugged to life. "Purrs like a kitten," she said and fell into the creamy chair, legs crooked over the armrest. She yawned in the sunlit spot, and soon sleep blew over her.

It was a quarter past canary seed when Onja jumped at Muktuk's warning welcome. She bolted to the window. A long, dark car skimmed over the hill from Stacy's farm. Like something from an old Batman movie, Onja thought. She ran down the stairs, grabbed the jean jacket from the banister and tripped out the front door. She stabilized herself at the end of the path and stood on a flat white rock, a keepsake from her mother's family homestead near Blooming, an hour's drive across the valley.

The dog was still barking, its front paws lifting off the ground.

"Quiet, Muktuk," Onja ordered the snarling black Lab.

The nose of the car bulleted up the lane. Onja hoped her dad was already out in the field; she couldn't hear the tractor.

Etthen parked and she ran to the passenger side. The dog wiggled and danced, grinning with all his teeth bared. Etthen remained in the car.

"Good morning," she croaked as she slammed the passenger door shut.

"Good morning." He turned, eyes on her as he reached his arm behind the black nylon seat, still cool to the touch in the early morning. Onja surveyed the car. The dash was faded black. An antique radio system with wide white knobs channeled Terri Clark's huskily feminine voice. Country? He didn't say he liked country, she remembered. But I did.

She glanced back at him, noting long sculpted arms, a wide chest beneath his black muscle shirt. His hair was pulled back behind his strong neck. Leigh was right. What a hotty!

He craned his neck a little more to see through the back window as he slid the transmission into reverse with his left hand. An adult body could have sat in the middle of the wide bench seat, but as he stretched toward her, eyes rolled to the side, the distance evaporated. His gentle breath. His straight teeth. A scar? She hadn't noticed that before. Just below the left side of his hairline there was a translucent seam in the shape of a lazy good-luck horseshoe.

He wheeled backward.

Onja glanced at the house and in her peripheral vision saw her dad watching from the cement pad in front of the garage. He raised his arm, hand upright, fingers rippling like spectators doing the wave at a Roughrider game. She threw her hand up and sent a weak smile.

Etthen returned his right arm to the wheel and jammed the accelerator with his foot. The farm disappeared in a tunnel cloud of dust. Dad's going to love this, Onja thought.

She turned to her window. The tug at her heart was new. It was as if she was leaving the farm for the first time. She packed a memory chest. The spent raspberry and saskatoon bushes lining the lane. The slough with ducks, mostly mallards, metallic green-headed drakes and their slightly larger dappled brown hens. Pintail pairs landed, trailing spiked feathers, leaving a *V* in the water. Small black mud hens ran along the surface before taking off. Ducklings, with only hints of fluff, played peek-a-boo among the cattails. A tuft of grass and weeds grew in a triangle at the foot of the lane.

Etthen turned right.

The freshly stoned road. The black cultivated earth. A resting field, shadowed with last year's stubble. The steep hill before the turn to Stacy's. The double-rutted trail announced with a circular grove of wolf willow and a pride of pussy willow. A border of agitated wild oats and shaking sweetgrass.

Now Etthen turned left.

A minute passed, then two. He turned toward the valley.

Soon the road rose over a small hill and down, then a bigger one, and another. The white Charolais cows in the community pasture on the horizon. Etthen slowed and turned onto an approach that led to the gate. He easily opened and closed it behind them, unlike that first time. They were one hill away from the double arched bridge, and alone with the indigenous pasture.

He drove much slower now, avoiding rocks and hollows; they still didn't speak. Onja busied her mind trying to name every plant she saw: sage, buffalo bills, brown-eyed Susans, cactus, buck brush, foxtail, orange and green moss, and there were more plants she didn't have names for. Why don't I ever ask Dad what kind of trees these are? Or are they just bushes? Is moss a plant? What are all these grasses called? Why is some sage tall and some so short? One of these days, she promised herself, I'll ask Dad to take me on a nature hike, and I'll have him name every plant I see.

Etthen crested the valley wall. Onja saw an old road twisting like snakes and ladders into the valley. "I've never been here before," she said.

"Hang on then," Etthen warned. He stepped on the gas and brought them onto the old road with rolling bumps and more dust. They followed until it opened onto the valley.

Canvas tarps and a huge tree drew their eyes across a rocky field of big round bales. He slowed and drove onto the valley floor, steering his way skillfully through the Druid-like obstacle course.

He honked his horn. Just like Grandpa used to, Onja thought.

A couple—wearing Panama hats, beige canvas shorts, beige button-up shirts with pockets on the chest—rose from the ground and waved, the man's smile as wide as the brim on his hat; the woman, tall and lithe, like a grassland dryad.

Etthen rolled down his window and called to the duo, "Where's Aniedi or Jones?"

The man under the huge hat pointed toward the river.

"What was that first name?" Onja asked gingerly.

"An—Yed—Eee." He emphasized the "yed" to rhyme with Jed. "And don't call her 'A—Need—Eee' or she'll let you have it."

"An—Yed—Eee," Onja practiced. "Isn't a Yeti another name for the Abominable Snowman or something?"

He turned his face toward hers. Briefly, his eyes seemed to look at a puzzle, piled piece over piece.

He paused, grasping the door handle. "By the way, I told them about the Kaffiyeh, and they might be disappointed you're only wearing a bandana."

Onja flushed.

He added, "You may want to wear that jean jacket. It's nippy out there this early." He opened his door and bounded from the car.

Onja watched. What was she supposed to do now?

In the Dirt

Onja sat alone in the car while Etthen sprinted toward the archaeologists. The man and woman pointed up the valley and down, across the river and back, toward the hills over which they'd driven. I've been dumped, she thought.

Onja startled. A rap on the window was like someone had yelled, "Boo." She turned to see a young woman with black skin and fancy button eyes. Her complexion is like the polished ebony on the crokinole board Thomas made for Dad, Onja thought. The woman knocked again, this time opening Onja's door. "Are you going to sit in there all day when there's work to do?"

"Uh, I guess not." Onja smiled shyly.

"Well, let's go then."

Onja reached to undo her seatbelt. The jean jacket—heavy as embarrassment—was still in her hands. Hope I wasn't cuddling it, she thought. She opened the door. Etthen was right; it was chilly, but there was no way she'd wear his jacket, especially if she might bump into his mom down here. She quickly placed it in the middle of the long seat and left the vehicle.

"Don't worry about Romeo…" Aniedi's voice was matter-of-fact. "He never goes too far."

They passed the tree and topped the riverbed wall; Onja gasped. Below them, stretching out on both sides of the river, a broken-up chessboard was carved into the earth. Huge squares, one meter by one meter, had been alternately dug or left as prairie. Either dark or light.

"This site is much larger than a usual Saskatchewan dig," Aniedi said. "Usually there would be a core crew of about five, with some volunteers showing up irregularly. But here we have two main trenches and a scatter of units out of sight of each other."

Beside the dark squares, which had been leveled at what Onja guessed was approximately ten centimeters, a group of crouching people lifted their heads and waved, then turned back to the dirt.

"Have you been to a dig before?"

"No, never."

Onja looked at Aniedi. Her eyes are a chocolate and caramel swirl, she thought, and her delicate lashes curl like smiles.

"Then you can come and help me at my unit."

"Sure." Onja paused. She panned her surroundings and noted Etthen walking toward the riverbed with the archaeologists. He could have at least told her where he was going. A growl edged her thoughts, but her mind snapped back like pulled elastic. "Are you 'An—Yed—Eee'?" She punched the "Yed."

"Sorry," Aniedi replied. "I could have introduced myself."

"That's okay. Etthen sort of told me who you are."

"He did?" Aniedi's voice mocked surprise, more girl now than grown-up. "What did he say?"

Onja looked back over her shoulder and lowered her voice. "He just told me not to say 'An—*Need*—Eee' or you'd give it to me."

Aniedi laughed, a giggly laugh. "I don't really care. Lots of people call me "An—Need—Eee." I just give *him* a hard time because, well, I don't know why, just because."

She laughed contagiously; Onja joined her.

"He's told me about you too, Onja."

Aniedi turned and started walking before Onja could respond. She saw that Aniedi's long braids were tied in a white bandana. The extensions patted Aniedi's back with every long stride. She wore mid-thigh khaki shorts, revealing long, lean legs, gray work socks, and brown hiking boots. Her long-sleeved, baggy white shirt was tucked in.

Onja followed Aniedi as she walked down the riverbed and onto the prairie squares. They passed a young man bent over a square of dark earth. On his cap, a drop, almost neon, was like a flash of orange oriole against blue trees.

Aniedi stopped and stood in profile against the backdrop of the valley. No wonder Etthen was asking for her, Onja thought; she's gorgeous. She didn't mean to stare, but there were no black people in Palliser. A few years ago, two of the Saskatchewan Roughriders—football players—visited her school, and they were black, but that was it.

"Here we are," Aniedi announced. "My spot."

Onja stopped staring and compassed the location. She noticed a handle protruding from the earth.

"That's a trowel," Aniedi said. "Standard issue in this sandy loam."

"Oh." Onja's right eyebrow raised in concentration.

Aniedi grinned. "I left my bucket where we sift the dirt." She pointed to a patch of chokecherry bushes. "Wait for me here, okay?"

Onja glanced back long enough to examine the last person they had passed. He was hunched over his square. The depression was level, except for a stalagmite protrusion which the young man wearing the Oilers cap was brushing with a long-bristled paintbrush. It reminded her of a miniature Big Muddy, where the wind polished sandstone rock into oddly shaped columns.

Aniedi returned with the bucket.

"What's he doing over there?" Onja asked as she pointed discreetly at their neighbor.

Aniedi paused. "We call that pedestaling. When you find something, like a bone or a projectile, you never pull it out. You continue digging, level by level, but you always leave the artifacts where you find them and excavate down in the rest of the unit. That way, when it's time to draw your floor plan, the relationships between the artifacts are clear."

"Cool," Onja said, eyes satisfied.

"Okay," Aniedi said as she knelt to the prairie. "Get over here and I'll show you how it's done." Aniedi picked up the

trowel and removed a thin layer of dirt, as if she were lev-
eling off the top of drying cement. She poured it into the
bucket. Then again, and again.

Onja coughed as debris puffed into the air.

Aniedi explained, "Each square is one meter by one
meter. We call this a *unit*. Each unit is divided into quarters,
or *quadrants*, as we call them. On this dig we're going down
five centimeters at a time. Sometimes you follow natural soil
levels, but here it's arbitrary. Five centimeters at a time."

Onja listened to Aniedi's authoritative voice. She wondered if Etthen had sat beside her, listening. Probably more
ogling than listening. Maybe leaning closer. Bumping up
against her arm. Onja looked around. No sign of him.

Aniedi had not stopped talking. "We have to collect all
the dirt from each site, sift it, catalog and bag any finds, and
then we return the leftovers to the same hole. We try to be
as non-intrusive as possible."

"As what?"

"We disturb as little as necessary."

Onja watched as Aniedi ran her fingers through the dirt,
as if she could taste the earth with her fingertips. "I get it."

"Nothing here but humus." Aniedi's voice was quiet.

"How often do you find something? Something interesting…"

"The curse of many sites is bags and bags of fire-cracked
rock from hearth fires and stone flakes from stone tools
being made or sharpened. Bone fragments and potsherds
come next in volume. Something spectacular is uncommon
to rare. Often there are no tools in a unit—but don't get me

wrong—everything is relevant and helps tell the story of what happened at this location when people lived there."

"What about whole bones?"

"They're not so routine, unless you're in a bone bed… then you find nothing but bison bones."

"What's a bone bed?"

"A kill site or a butchering site. Now that's tedious. But down here, a good day might bring in a dog tooth or two, and maybe once a week I find a projectile point."

"Do you mean an arrowhead?"

Aniedi bobbed her head.

"My dad has lots of those."

"Don't tell anyone around here," Aniedi stage-whispered and looked from side to side. "He's not really supposed to keep projectile points unless he has a permit or registers them."

Onja gulped dryly.

Aniedi laughed. "Don't worry about it. There aren't any heritage police after people's collections, and it's not like the museums want people to turn over every point and bone picked up either. The point of our heritage regulations is to encourage people to leave artifacts where they are unless they surface-collect with a purpose to collect and share provenance and other data on their finds."

Onja nodded.

Aniedi drew circles in the remaining dirt. "So, has your family lived near the valley for a long time?"

"I guess so. My great-great-grandfather Claibourn home-steaded two of the four quarters in our quarter section."

"Wow." Aniedi's dark eyes brightened. "I wish he was still around."

"My great-great-grandpa? Yes, I never met him either. But I met my great-grandpa. Well…I guess he met me, but he died at ninety-eight, when I was six months old."

"So would that make West Claibourn your grandfather?"

"Oh, no. He's my great-uncle."

"What about your grandpa?"

Aniedi's eyes relaxed as Onja paused.

"Grandpa died last winter."

Aniedi hummed an empathetic "hmmm" and then spoke wistfully. "I'm sure he had lots of stories about this valley."

Onja looked up at the hills and then down the valley. "My great-grandma MacLeod was the first baby born in this area…"

"You mean the first *white* baby?"

Onja paused. "Yes, that's what I meant." She sat back on her haunches. "When my great-grandma got married, the Indians left a side of deer in a tree as a wedding present."

Aniedi's eyes widened and she made an "uh" sound as her jaw dropped. "You're kidding."

"Nope," Onja replied slowly, "true story."

A Cooper's hawk surveyed the landscape from above. Onja and Aniedi watched the bird until it melted into the hazy sky.

Aniedi sighed. "This archaeology is dirty, dusty work. The days are long and hot, and for what? A bone, a fire stone, a voiceless piece of history. But just that little story, a deer in a tree, now that's *living* history. Stories. I love stories." Her face was a rainbow of expression.

"But why would you want to know stories about *this* valley?"

"Why wouldn't I?" Aniedi swatted a fly away from her face.

"Wouldn't Egypt or Mesopotamia be more interesting?"

The young archaeologist laughed a high, musical laugh. "Mesopotamia? Egypt? Everyone's already heard those stories. This valley has untold stories. Doesn't that make it more interesting?"

"I guess so." Onja shrugged, remembering that her dad had said almost the same thing.

"Look at us daydreaming," Aniedi scolded playfully. "Here, you take a turn."

By the River

Aniedi let Onja do most of the troweling and sifting that morning. It was a good day. They found a dogtooth and a small shard of pottery. The earthenware was a rusty gray with a pinched design along one edge. Aniedi said that it was from the rim of a bowl. "Julia will flip her lid," she told Onja as she turned the shard over. "I think we've found some pot scum."

"Some what?" Onja laughed.

Aniedi explained that one of the women on the team was studying cooking residue, literally pot scum. She already had conclusive evidence that the First People who frequented this valley were trading for corn from as far south as the Dakotas. And the styles of pottery were beginning to connect the people more with southern groups, like the Hidatsa and Mandan, rather than only the Plains Cree and Nakota.

They placed each specimen in a tiny square plastic bag with a tag listing site, unit, quadrant and researcher. Aniedi asked how to spell Onja and then wrote "Onja and Aniedi" onto each card.

Onja's notion of only-in-Egypt archaeology faded as the sun climbed higher into the cloudless sky.

Aniedi had done most of the talking. She had finished a degree in history and was now working toward a master's degree in cultural anthropology. She was considering writing her thesis using stories from this valley. Onja hadn't known such a thing was even possible, and she'd never met anyone who seemed more interested in her valley.

Onja wiped a bead of sweat off her forehead with the back of her wrist.

The sun is like a heat lamp high in the sky, she thought.

"Time for lunch," Aniedi announced.

Onja straightened from her crouching position.

"Onja," Aniedi's expression was serious, "do you think you'd come with me to talk to some of the old-timers in this area about the valley?"

"Ah, sure," Onja said.

"Great." Aniedi looked around at the other sites. "They've beaten us back to the camp. Let's go."

They retraced their path. Onja noticed the tools cast haphazardly—like bone fragments—beside each unit: trowel, brush, bucket. Had they been there before? Her imagination exploded. If a meteor hit the earth right now, covering everything with ash, what would future archaeologists think of this? It's like a mirror inside a mirror.

After climbing up the riverbed wall and back to the vehicles, Aniedi led Onja to a wash center—complete with water bucket, soap and towels—shaded under a blue tarp. Onja followed Aniedi's example and scrubbed her hands, gasping at the first splash of water on her face.

It was warm, but it cooled and refreshed just the same.

Aniedi then took Onja to a jeep, opened the hatch and reached for a bottle of lotion. "I should have made you put this on earlier. You're a little pink."

"I did put some on this morning," Onja said.

Aniedi squirted some into her own hands and rubbed the liquid onto her dusty legs. "Here, you do the same."

Onja followed her instructions. She looked at her own white skin and across at Aniedi's black skin. I didn't know she would need to wear sunscreen, Onja thought.

Aniedi took the lotion and rubbed a little onto the back of Onja's neck.

"You should have had some of this too." Aniedi handed Onja a bottle of water. "There's no ice," Aniedi explained. "It's not good for you to drink really cold water in this kind of sun."

Onja squinted, her eyes peeking out behind long lashes. When had the nippy morning turned to a sweltering afternoon?

"Let's eat." Aniedi pulled two small brown paper bags from a cooler. "You're lucky. Two of our gang went to town. Look what they left for you." She handed one to Onja.

Onja smiled. She hadn't thought to pack a lunch.

The archaeology team was eating either in the shade of the tree or under the tarp. They sat in groups of three and four. Most of them looked about Aniedi's age; probably in their early twenties, Onja thought. Everyone wore head coverings—some ball caps, others bandanas.

She saw Etthen sitting with the professionals. She'd almost forgotten him! She tried to look casual as she scoped the other groups and evaluated the women to determine if any could be Etthen's mother. They were all too young and too fair. But, Onja thought, my cousins aren't dark like their mom, Auntie Naomi, who's from Jamaica. Maybe Etthen's mom is white. She studied the women again. Nope. They were all too young.

Onja's eyes skirted the archaeologists under the Panama hats. I'll bet they have British accents to match their costumes, she thought. Nobody has told them they're in the Little Mouse Valley of southern Saskatchewan. No pyramids here.

Onja took in the rest of the team as she followed Aniedi. Other than Aniedi, they all looked like Caucasians with really good tans.

Onja wondered how many black people had been in the valley before. In grade five she had found a short book in her mother's bedroom called *North to Freedom*. She remembered lying on the floor reading the story of Harriet Tubman over and over. Her code name was Moses and she'd sing, "Tell old Pharaoh, to let my people go" in a muscular voice as she walked through a village. This told people she was ready to make a run for Canada. Onja's heart stirred with maple-leaf pride. "Oh, Canada, glorious and free," she thought.

The Little Mouse River was only fifteen miles from the US border. Onja had never considered that maybe slaves had followed the North Star, and the little woman with the deep voice, right through her valley on the way to freedom.

Aniedi sat a little apart from a young woman and two guys. She patted the ground beside her. "Have a seat," she added, turning to the nearest group. "This is Onja, my slave for the morning."

Onja paled, an ironic twist in her gut. She diverted her focus and met Etthen's smile. He turned back to his conversation with the archaeologists.

Aniedi opened her lunch, leaned against the tree and gazed into the hills.

Onja sat too, opened her lunch bag, but she let her eyes follow the noontime talk.

"It's all political," the woman in the fishing cap said. "I was reading an article in *Earth River Report* titled 'Build Now, Worry Later.'"

"That sums it up. Wise and his boys know what they want. They want votes, and this dam is their ticket." It was the Oilers cap guy. He sounds like he knows what he's talking about, Onja thought.

"It's all about selling Canada off to the Americans. When Big Brother barks, we jump," another guy, wearing baggy earth-colored clothing, chimed in.

Which one is Etthen's conspiracy-theory guy? she wondered. What was his name again? Oh yeah, Jones.

"You know, I'm sick of everyone demonizing the Americans," a young woman with a checked bandana said. "Did you know, just over there along the forty-ninth parallel, Saskatchewanians and Albertans refused entry to Oklahoma blacks at the turn of the last century? You should read what the newspapers said about black immigrants."

"You're changing the topic," Oilers Cap said sternly.

"No, I'm not. You're the one going on about the

Americans, as though they're always the bad guys. Did you know Saskatchewan had one of the biggest KKK presences in Canada? And Canada had black slaves?"

Onja tore at the cool prairie grass. It was almost coarse enough to rip her skin. She continued listening, eyes down. She nibbled the sandwich but wasn't hungry.

"Like I was saying," Oilers Cap continued, "it's the Old Man and James Bay all over again. This dam is right up there."

"No kidding."

"You'd think the public would ask some questions, but most people around here think it's a good thing. Remember the street dance?" the Oilers fan said, stirring Onja's memory. I could have gone to that dance, if I wasn't too chicken to go alone, she recalled. And then Stacy—who had said she didn't want to go—went anyway…without me. Anger, like a dash of pepper, spiced Onja's mood.

"Yeah, that was something else. Most places there'd be people protesting. Here—they're dancing in the streets."

"Except for those brothers, they've kicked up a little stink. But who's listening?"

I'm listening, Onja thought.

A man in the group closest to Onja interrupted. "Lighten up, Jones. Who do you think's paying your way down here? If it's so evil, why don't you quit?"

"Yeah," said the checked-bandana woman.

Onja made the connection: Jones was Oilers Cap Guy. She peeked in time to see his eyes flash in the direction of his challenger. He didn't say anything. Onja turned to the grass.

Another group was laughing.

"And then he bent over…"

"And then…"

"Let's just say we heard a rumbling that hasn't been heard on these plains since the Folsom spear landed in a woolly mammoth."

There was a new explosion of laughter.

In between gasps, someone said, "Must be all the grazing on fresh vegetables."

Onja lifted her face. The entire team was now either laughing uncontrollably or smiling condescendingly, all except Jones. Either way, all conversations ended.

Etthen had a huge grin dividing his face. He stood, held his hands behind his back and stretched. Ouch, Onja thought. I feel every crack. He walked outside of the shade and plunked himself down beside Aniedi.

"Hey, junior," she said.

"Hi, 'An—Yed—Eee.'" He leaned forward. "Onja, they want to know if you want an official tour this afternoon." He nodded toward the archaeologists.

"Sure." Onja was quick to answer.

Etthen sat back against the tree and cuddled into Aniedi's side.

Aniedi stood up abruptly. "You are as annoying as my little brother, and that's annoying!"

Onja tried to see Etthen through Aniedi's eyes, see a silly boy. It wasn't too hard now that he was hanging his head and rolling it around like a scolded puppy. But when he stood up and laughed, he looked all man.

Onja stood alongside the others. The archaeologists appeared at her side. When had they moved?

The man spoke. "Etthen, are you going to introduce us?"

"Sure. Roy and Verna, this is Onja. *O—N—J*, as in Jack—*A*."

He gave Onja a sideways glance and raised his eyebrows twice, like a corny comedian, Onja thought. "She lives on the farm next to where Mom and I are staying." Then he turned to Onja. "The man under the fedora is Roy, but I like to call him Indy."

Onja shook hands with Roy. "Pleased to meet you."

Etthen continued, "And this is Verna."

Onja shook hands again. "Hi."

Verna spoke in a flat, academic voice. "Did you enjoy the morning?"

So much for the British accent, Onja thought. "I sure did," she blurted and then examined the ground, embarrassed by her own enthusiasm.

Verna chuckled. "Great!" Her voice spiked to match Onja's. "Roy and I are going to MacLeod Lake this afternoon." She pointed east along the valley. "We thought you and Etthen might like to tag along."

MacLeod Lake, Onja thought, that's near Uncle West's. I wonder if they know it was named after my great-great-grandparents?

Roy continued, "We're setting up a new dig site. That's always fun."

Onja smiled her agreement, not trusting herself to speak again.

Aniedi took a step and then turned. "Have a fun afternoon, Onja. Come back anytime. Good help is hard to find."

Onja's mouth curved into her half-baked smile as the others chuckled.

Aniedi added, "Remember what we talked about."

"Sure," Onja stammered.

Aniedi crumpled her lunch bag and tossed it into a garbage bin beside the jeep. "Look at this," she called over her shoulder to anyone listening. "I'm the last to lunch and the first back to work."

"If we don't want to be outdone by Aniedi—again—we had better get going," Verna announced, loud enough for Aniedi to hear. "Let's take my jeep."

"Onja," Etthen said, "I want you to meet one more person."

Onja glanced at Jones.

"I see you've already figured out who he is." Etthen followed Onja's eyes. "He does make an impression, you've got to give him that."

Onja followed Etthen back under the shady tarp. "Jones, this is Onja Claibourn, a friend of mine."

Oilers Cap Guy shot Onja a laser glare from under the beak of his cap. "What relation to West Claibourn?"

Onja frowned. What's with the Uncle West interrogation? she thought. "He's my great-uncle."

"Great's a matter of perspective," Jones said.

"Okay, nice meeting you too," Etthen said. "We need to go now." He crooked Onja's arm in his and escorted her toward the waiting archaeologists. "Okay, that was weird, but that's why you gotta love the guy. He's always on the edge."

Yeah, and maybe he needs a little push *off* the edge, Onja thought. *Jerk.*

The back of the jeep was full of coolers and water, as well as scrolled maps, worn booklets, dusty binders, loose pens and sharp pencils.

"Just push that stuff to the side, or toss it into the back," Roy advised.

They backed out of the campsite and renegotiated the obstacle course of giant bales and fieldstones to lead them out of the valley. Onja dared a glance at Etthen, who was daring a glance at her too.

Through a Cactus Patch

Cool air was just reaching the backseat when Verna drove the jeep off the valley flat and up the trail. Onja raised the water bottle to her lips and took enough for one swallow. She let her eyes drift into the no-man's-land of the middle seat, but Etthen's face was against the window.

She watched the rolling landscape. It was like meeting new uncles and aunts she hadn't grown up with: crow's-feet pinching happy blue eyes, women with thin lips, men with bald heads. So new, but so much the same.

Onja tried to decode the conversation in the front seat. If they went an inch, it would be a thousand years. Two inches, two thousand. If they pulled people from this site, they could go further in the new, unnamed site.

She slowly brought her mind and gaze into the vehicle. Etthen was looking at her, unapologetically, almost impolitely. His face was stern, like an athlete preparing for competition. He had arrows of black whiskers along his upper lip pointing to ruddy lips below. The hollow of his cheek was like the nest left in a morning pillow, Onja thought.

She met his searching gaze, wondering if she was being sized up. Measuring in return.

She looked away, angry with herself for saying she had a boyfriend. Victor. What kind of name was that anyway? Sounds like a vampire! There's no way he believes that a plain Jane like me could have a boyfriend, she thought. I bet he's already guessed that I lied.

After driving slowly for about fifteen minutes on the prairie trail, Verna turned onto a freshly graveled road. The grinding of stone on stone sounded like running water.

"There's no way they should have planted those in this soil," Roy said, pointing through the front window. Tiny evergreen trees in dark cultivated rows grew along each side of the road. Looks silly on the native grassland, Onja thought. The jeep dipped into the first roll toward the valley. Ahead an erratic rock loomed, like a giant tombstone. Twig trees had been planted between brown picnic tables.

Onja was alarmed. It was like seeing picnic tables in her own pasture. The painted wood against the sage and prairie grasses just didn't seem right. There were deciduous saplings in dark, newly dug earth, making one big circle around the misplaced park.

Beyond the disturbed land and down the valley wall, a long, narrow lake mimicked the blue sky. An elm tree grew on the west side, stretching upward.

Verna pulled up beside the rock. Roy was the first out of the jeep.

Onja knew she was still in the valley, not many miles from her farm, but she felt as if she'd just landed on the moon. What was this place? Picnic tables? A lake? That can't be MacLeod Lake, Onja thought.

Roy led the way toward the rock. "Here's the beginnings of eco tourism, Palliser Triangle style. Have you heard of the Palliser Triangle?" he asked Onja.

She nodded. After all, she went to Palliser School.

"I haven't heard of it," Etthen said behind them.

Roy turned to Etthen. "Palliser was an early surveyor sent west by the government in the mid-1880s to decide if this land could support settlers."

"Funny thing they needed a European to determine if this land, which has supported people for eons, was viable." Verna and Roy exchanged a rueful glance.

Roy continued, "Palliser declared portions of southern Alberta, Saskatchewan and Manitoba to be semi-arid or at least dry sub-humid. Today they talk about combating desertification, which is the process of an ecosystem turning into desert. That's one of the rallying cries behind the urgency to flood this valley."

"Wasn't it John Macoun who rethought Palliser's prediction and said this land could be farmed?" Onja asked, though she already knew the answer. She had written a research paper in grade seven titled "John

Macoun: Unsung Saskatchewan Hero."

"Hey, you know your history." Verna patted Onja on the shoulder. She added, "Yes, John Macoun was a naturalist. His scientific authority opened up the Palliser Triangle. Funny they didn't name it the Macoun Triangle."

Onja beamed. How many times have I wished they had named Palliser 'Macoun'? Palliser is so negative, the voice of doom and gloom. Macoun? He was an optimist.

Onja gloated. *I like Verna.*

Roy smiled and continued, "This part of Saskatchewan has always been concerned with water. Ever since the thirties there have been water management boards. A dam has always been on the agenda, but this dream to set up a water park is something new. Here are the beginnings."

They walked to the huge rock. Facing the valley, engraved in the blue granite, were the blackened words *MacLeod Heritage Park* and below that *In Memory of Samuel and Ella MacLeod, 1893*. Onja stepped forward and placed her hand on the warm surface, tracing the grooves. These are my people, she thought. The sun pressed down, holding her fingers and palm against the stone.

Roy continued his history lesson. "Do you see that farmhouse on this side of the valley?"

Their eyes followed his outstretched arm.

"Just across from the house on the other side of the river are the remains of a stone barn. That was the old MacLeod ranch."

Onja interrupted, "Grandpa MacLeod, Samuel, came from Ontario, and Grandma Ella was Pennsylvania Dutch."

Roy, Verna and Etthen turned to look at Onja.

Onja felt light-headed, as if she were waking from a dream.

"That's Uncle West's ranch house down there. Ella and Samuel MacLeod were Uncle West's grandparents, my great-great-grandparents."

"You're certainly connected, Onja," Roy said. "This was one of the first homesteads in the valley."

This park was a museum. Roy's voice was the pleasant electronic interpreter. He was explaining her people to the world. Onja didn't know if she was part of the exhibit or an observer.

She itched with questions. Why didn't she know about this park? When was it built? Other questions popped out: "Why did they build the park up here? Wouldn't it have been better right at the ranch?"

Verna scrutinized Onja's expectant face, then answered simply, "Because the dam will eventually flood the valley. That ranch will be under fifteen meters of water."

Onja's muscles tensed in disbelief. She wanted to blurt, "Screw the dam," but the sun pinned her, still and unmovable. She tried to imagine the dry valley below with anything more than a weak, narrow river snaking a pitiful stream of water that couldn't even fill the riverbed on the valley floor.

Impossible, she thought confidently, absolutely impossible. Think like Macoun. Be an optimist.

A soft roar. Onja turned her head; when did Verna return to the jeep? She saw Roy open his door.

Etthen called, "We want to walk down. We'll be right behind you."

Onja stood at attention, hands at her side, rock to her back. A blow-dryer of wind tossed a strand of hair the color of wild oats across her eyes. She tucked it behind her ear.

She slumped back against the boulder. The government was really planning a dam. More than planning; they were acting on their plans. A shot of pain burned across the back of her neck. Must have missed sunscreen on a strip, Onja thought. She shivered in the early afternoon heat.

Etthen had started across the undisturbed prairie toward the long lake.

"It's impossible, you know," Onja called after him, snapping from her trance.

He turned. "What's impossible?"

"Flooding this valley. They can build their dam, but they can't make the water come."

"You sound like the gang outside Noah's ark. Can't you see the rain clouds coming?"

Onja looked at the hazy hot sky. "There's not a cloud in sight."

"That's what Noah's buddies thought too, and look what happened to them."

Onja remembered the story of Noah's ark from Sunday school. She had always identified with the people in the ark, the believers, not the others. This time, she was an other. Sure, God could flood the valley, but she had no faith in a man-made flood.

She ran to catch up with Etthen. "Nope," she said confidently as they stepped carefully through a cactus patch, "it's just not going to happen."

In Archaeology 101

Onja and Etthen climbed onto the telephone poles bridging the Little Mouse River and paced up the riverbed and over a bank. They found the archaeologists hunched over a piece of rusted metal that poked from the base of a shack.

Etthen coughed. "Hmm hmm."

"What took you so long?" Roy said without lifting his head from the treasure.

"Oh, Onja was just filling me in on Palliser and…what was that guy's name? Cocoon?"

"It's Macoun." Onja quietly defended her hero.

"How do you like the view?" Etthen asked.

Onja didn't answer. It's like déjà vu, she thought. But something's different. She had never approached Uncle West's ranch from this direction—there were pastures, fences, farms and prairie trails between her farm and Uncle West's.

"So, Indy, are you going to give Onja the Archaeology 101 tour?" Etthen glanced at Onja. She tilted her head slightly and pursed her lips.

"Of course," Roy answered, standing up. "I've got a captive audience and we need to scout this place some more anyway."

Roy held his arms crooked, palms upward, and began. "Archaeology is the exploration of human history. Wherever people have lived, they have left behind clues. Our job is to locate, detail and interpret." His hands, slowly moving outward, presented the farmyard.

Verna threw her voice from the grass. "A lot of people confuse us with dinosaur hunters."

"Paleontologists?" Etthen asked on cue.

Verna nodded. "The only way we would care about a T-Rex is if we were the first to find knife lacerations on his ancient bones." She lifted her face as if sensing a change in the weather. "And that's an impossible *if*. The only mammal at the time of the Terrible Lizard was a hairy little rodent. Maybe Roy's ancestor, but not mine."

Etthen and Onja looked at Roy. He doesn't seem the comeback kind of guy, Onja thought. Etthen said, "Nothing fazes you, hey, Indy?"

Roy walked to the other side of the weathered building. He steadied his foot on an upturned tin bucket and rested his hands on his knee. "The first thing we did when we came to this valley was identify the sites...any place where people left their lifestyle fingerprints."

Verna joined him. "We call those fingerprints 'artifacts'. Anything qualifies that has been created or modified by people, like the obvious projectile points, tin cans and scraped bones. But even rocks in a field can make an archaeologist look twice if they have been arranged in a circle or line."

"Like medicine wheels and buffalo runs," Onja interrupted.

"You bet." Verna pulled the brim of her hat down slightly.

Onja looked up at the hills. She remembered her father showing her tipi rings above Stony Crossing. In grade three she had gathered stones from all over the pasture and built a fire ring and a tipi ring. She remembered pouting for days when her father told her she couldn't light a fire, but she and her cousins still slept outside in the tipi ring.

Those rings of home had piqued her curiosity. Who were those people? She dreamed of invisible time travel where she could visit their camp without them knowing.

Mrs. Durham, her grade four teacher, had put names into these dreams: Nakota, Lakota, Cree, Siksika, Saulteaux and the northern Dene. Mrs. Durham was Métis herself and had taken them on hikes, pointing out a variety of plants. Onja remembered that Mrs. Durham had said the plantain's wide leaves could be used to aid in healing a cut.

"We locate sites in a variety of ways," Roy said. "Sometimes farmers, ranchers, miners, people whose jobs take them outside stumble onto a useful site, but usually archaeologists are seeking sites. We walk side by side, perhaps five meters apart, watching for any telltale signs on the surface, or maybe something exposed by nature, like a badger hole or erosion."

"Sometimes old maps might prompt a dig. Every situation is a little different," Verna added.

Roy and Verna walked ahead toward the river. Etthen put his arm around Onja. "I like to think of this as *payback* for that little lecture on Palliser and Cocoon up in the park." He squeezed her shoulder, dropped his arm and followed the tour guides.

"That's *Ma*—coun," she said, with phony rage. She carried his imprint like a sport embroidered on the sleeve of a high school jacket.

Verna had stopped and was swimming her hand through the grass as though looking for something she'd lost. Roy waited at the top of the riverbank. "We've already taken inventory and marked our maps. This is an important site because we'll study turn-of-the-century life; we won't look any deeper than that, unless we get a surprise."

Verna continued her fishing. "Even going back those hundred years will be time-consuming and costly because we must articulate specific records on each quadrant, and in doing so, we possibly contaminate data which could be useful to colleagues in the future."

Roy bent down to tie his boot. "Not every homestead in this valley will be excavated, and even those we do excavate are rarely fully excavated. When we go in, there has to be a specific problem we are trying to solve."

Verna stood and brushed twice at her khaki shorts. "For example, our research question for this site is, 'What was the extent and usage of purchased goods compared to homegrown supplies in the early 1900s?'"

Verna glanced at Roy, their eyes locking for a moment.

Roy pushed on his knees to stand up. "When archaeological sites are in danger—like each one in this valley is—we want to go into as much detail as we can; however, that just isn't always practical."

"It's all about picking and choosing. But it breaks my heart to leave so much behind." Verna crouched to the ground again. "We do what we can with what we're given. Our records may be all that are saved for now."

"What do you mean, 'for now'?" Onja stumbled into the question.

"Well, nothing is forever. Archaeologists will be back in here, some day," Roy said. "A flooded valley won't wreck everything below."

Onja looked up and then side to side. She tried to imagine water all around her. Pushing against her. Things just don't change like that, she thought.

The tag-team lecture continued: dating a site, after excavation, protection of archaeological materials in Saskatchewan.

Verna pointed at a depression in the land that had been a settler's home. A stone base was all that remained of a barn.

Friday, August 3
Dear Stacy,

I know you probably haven't received my last snail mail. I don't know when Mom and Dad are going to enter this millennium and get a computer. In September I'll be able to e-mail from school.

Why didn't you tell me about the Mercredis renting your farm? Was it a secret? Did you even know?

I'm sort of getting to know Etthen, the guy who helped me after my fall. He's really sweet in a big brother kind of way. Not that my brother is sweet, but you know what I mean. I gave his jean jacket back. I wanted to keep it, but that would have been too cheeseball, sort of a pathetic cry for attention, don't you think? He told me he has a girlfriend up north. It's kind of cool that he has a girlfriend because then he won't think I'm interested. It's still fun to dream. Ugh. I'm starting to gross myself out. (I can't believe I told you all that.)

Etthen has his driver's license. He took me to an archaeology dig in the valley. Yes, *this* valley! Apparently his mom is one of the archaeologists, but I haven't met her yet.

Did you know about all this archaeology stuff? There are archaeologists running all over, talking about First People or First Nations or Aboriginals. (I've always just said Indian, but I get the feeling that's a bad word or something.)

I feel so stupid not knowing anything about this. It's, like, fifteen minutes from the farm. They are taking this whole damn thing (ha) pretty seriously too, but I really don't think they can hurt anything. It's the water that I would be worried about, *if* I was worried, but I'm sure the valley could never flood. I'll eat my Kaffiyeh if it does.

Still, when we were talking with Roy and Verna (two of the archaeologists), it was freaking me out. Roy said that the government is spending thousands, probably millions, for them to do their research. He called it a trade-off. He doesn't really want the valley to be flooded because it would cover all that history, but if it wasn't being flooded, then there wouldn't be any money for the research. He called it a "Catch 22."

Sorry, there I go obsessing about the valley.

Yesterday was pretty cool because Etthen and I walked all the way from this little park (that's another story) at the top of the valley, down to MacLeod Lake. (Have you ever been there?) The first hill was really steep, and a couple of times I sort of bumped into his arm. How can a person get goose bumps when it's over thirty degrees Celsius?

Have you met any guys in Medicine Hat?

I'm going to invite Etthen for a ride to the pump house. I wonder if the Fosters would lend him one of their horses? Maybe we'll even pack a picnic. Dream, dream, dream…

I met this amazing lady named Aniedi who is working at the dig, sort of a junior archaeologist. She asked me if I'd take her around—actually, she'll take *me* around—to visit some of the old-timers because she's writing about stories from the valley. I'm sure if Etthen finds out, he'll want to come…I think he has a major crush on her.

Sounds like a Palliser love triangle! Ha.

Take it easy!

Your best friend,

Onja

P.S. When does school start for you? We go back Wednesday, August 29. I hate going back before September.

P.P.S. When I was helping at the dig I burned the back of my neck. Just call me a redneck! Ha.

P.P.P.S. Can't wait to hear from you!!

P.P.P.P.S. There was no trade-off for me when you left. Just my big broken heart!

Onja flopped onto her bed and hugged a pillow. Superman soared above. The blue of his eyes was faded in the indirect sunlight. She reread her letter to Stacy, folded it in half, then into thirds. Her eyes were heavy, like shade after sun.

She pointed her toes and crunched to sit up, the letter tight in her hand. An addressed envelope waited on the desk. She licked the bitter film and tasted iron on her tongue.

"Ouch!" A paper cut stung her lip.

On the Way To Town

Onja left her basement bedroom carrying the envelope addressed to Stacy. "Mom," she called from halfway up the stairs, "do you have a stamp?"

Onja's mother walked out of her bedroom across from the library. After digging in her purse, she handed Onja a stamp with the queen on it.

"Don't you have a fancy stamp? This one is so boring." She handed the stamp back.

"Your dad's going into town for parts. Why don't you go with him? Then you can buy whatever stamp meets your fancy requirements."

Onja took a juice box from the pantry and trotted down the stairs, slipping on sandals before stepping outside.

"That's not much for breakfast," Sylvia called just as Onja shut the door.

No clouds. No rain. Onja was not surprised to hear her father clanging metal on metal underneath the nearly extinct bailer.

"You could give me a hand here." His cracking voice was like thunder three seconds after lightning. "Pass me that wrench."

Onja's voice was harsh but quiet. "What wrench?"

"The crescent wrench…by the tractor." His voice maintained its intensity.

"Where?" Onja twisted her neck toward the orange Massey-Harris.

"By the back wheel!" he yelled, tension arching between each word.

Onja found the wrench tossed on a parched, dirt-caked patch of earth, bordered by an ankle-high cluster of prairie rose—petals pale pink, frightened by the relentless summer sun, Onja thought. She retrieved the crescent wrench and ambled back to her dad. "Here you go." He reached for it, then disappeared under the bailer again.

She heard the screen door squeak open. "Onja, here's a list," Sylvia called. "Can you pick up a few things while your dad's in the shop? Just charge everything."

"Sure." Onja turned from her father and met her mother on the white stone walkway. Sylvia's toenails were like scarlet flowers, blooming from her Birkenstocks. She waved the list: one third of a page torn lengthwise.

Onja studied the scrawl. "Mom, I haven't got a clue what…"

"Sweetened condensed milk," Sylvia said.

Onja's eyes continued to study the artsy curves on the page. "I hate it when he gets like this. No wonder Thomas moved to Alberta."

"That's not why he left, dear," her mother said. "It's a tough time of year for your father. He's got a lot on his mind as he gets ready for harvest. Will it rain before the crops burn? Before he gets the bales in?"

"I know, I know...I just wish he wouldn't yell."

Sylvia raised her eyebrows and Onja turned in time to see her father emerge, smiling now, from beneath the bailer. "I think I can make this thing last another year," he announced.

Onja turned and whispered to her mother, "Dr. Jekyll or Mr. Hyde?"

"Who's coming to town?" Wayne asked cheerfully. He was already halfway to the truck.

Onja strode toward the rusting red GMC and climbed in. Wayne adjusted the sun visor. Dirt and oil highlighted the lifelines on his palm. His thumb against the key in the ignition was capped with a blue and purple moon. Nicks and scrapes edited his hands, like an English teacher's red pen gone mad, Onja thought. *Note to self: Don't marry a farmer!*

Wayne looked quickly around, honked the horn and backed out of the yard. When he was a young hired man at a neighbor's farm, he'd saved a little girl's life. He'd watched the driver climb into the cab of a grain truck and start it up. Then he noticed the child playing right beside the big rear wheels. He had run and scooped her up—like Superman— just as the truck had plunged into reverse.

She examined his hands again as the truck passed the apple and cherry trees. Hands that made porridge in the morning. Hands that scratched math problems in metric and imperial. Hands that scrubbed dishes. Hands that built a tire swing. Her father's hands picked saskatoons and raspberries with two pails hanging on belts around his neck. Onja looked at her hands. She was proud if she could pick one pail to his two.

She wondered what her dad thought as he drove past his trees and orchard. She remembered riding on a borrowed tree-planter, plunking baby Manitoba maples into the ground. Now look at them, she thought whimsically. They're all grown up.

Wayne turned left at the end of the lane, toward Palliser.

"So, how was your field trip?" he asked.

"It was okay."

"Just okay?"

"Do you know about MacLeod Park?"

"Sure, I ordered the trees for them from Indian Head. Thomas and I helped plant them this spring. Why?"

"How come I've never heard about it? Is it some big secret or something?"

"It's no secret. You know that Samuel and Ella MacLeod were your great-great-grandparents."

"Well, yeah…" Onja scrunched her eyebrows and narrowed her eyes. What other secrets are lurking in that valley? she wondered. She didn't know if she felt angry or proud. Angry to find out her father knew all about the changes, or proud to have a park named for her family. Maybe she'd have to invent a new word for the emotion she was feeling: Prang? Groud?

Her father continued, "I know MacLeod Lake like the back of my hand. I used to visit Great-Grandma there when I was young, and I've hunted every inch of that valley."

"Doesn't it bother you they're planning to flood it?"

Wayne looked across the vehicle at his oldest daughter. His expression is either hostile or hurt, Onja thought. It was like he was saying *What do you think*?

She turned her gaze outside and imagined away the grayish brown mustard field, remembering the cheerful yellow bloom that had invited the drive to Palliser before she had left for camp; just two weeks ago, the valley had been hers. Hers alone. No archaeologists. No relatives. No Dad. And no Etthen. Could she get used to sharing? Well…maybe, she thought. It was weird—these newcomers were there for all the wrong reasons. All in the name of flooding the valley. Her valley: yes, it was still *her* valley.

Her eyes bounced from black flax on the right to bearded barley on the left.

It just will never happen and that's all there is to it, Onja calmed herself. They can believe what they want. In fact, I'm glad they think it will flood. I'm learning about my valley. I'm meeting interesting people. Too bad they're here on false hope, she thought.

Onja sat quietly as the miles ticked by on the standard odometer. She didn't even know exactly how many kilometers it was to town. They always said *six miles*. Metric vs. imperial. I wasn't even born when the government decided to officially change our measurement system, and we still don't get it. Well, except on highway trips we measure in metric. Height: feet and inches. Milk and ice cream: liters. Weight: pounds. Triple-jump: meters. Cooking: cups and teaspoons. One system or the other, it was the same distance to town, she thought. Why did the government have to change things?

As they pulled up to the highway, her father slowed and steered slightly to the right, then he wheeled tight to the left and came to a stop. Onja called this a farmer stop. Dad said it was a hand-me-down from driving big trucks with boxes. This way they could see to either side of the road before crossing. Onja thought it was cool. Kind of like getting off her horse by swinging her right leg over Ginger's head. It's all about the little things that nobody thinks much about, Onja thought. That's what makes life fun.

They waited for a semi to pass, then crossed the highway into the village of Palliser. "Dad," Onja said, "when did Uncle West move to Stephan?"

"Early last year. Why?"

"I was just out at the ranch site yesterday and it felt like a ghost town." She tried to conjure a memory of the ranch before yesterday. Etthen's arm around her shoulder and Roy and Verna's professor voices filled the hollow in her mind.

They pulled up to the Palliser Co-op and post office, a newly constructed white building with red trim that had replaced the old Co-op store with its authentic false front, just like in the Old West movies. The green street sign read *Ciaro*, although at the other end it was *Cairo*. *Small-town Saskatchewan*, she'd heard her mother lament. *I'll pay for a new sign at one end, if they'd just decide Ciaro or Cairo!* Onja didn't tell her mother that another street was named Wolf and Wolfe and another Oumiette and Omiet. She might go broke just buying street signs, Onja mused.

Her father hurried up the concrete steps and into the hardware half of the store. Onja followed at a slower pace and entered the post office. There was a familiar face at the counter.

"Hi, Onja," Aniedi said. She embraced a brown package to her chest as if she held the secret to world peace.

"Hi, Aniedi," Onja replied while scanning Aniedi, the envelope and her mail key.

"I'm so excited! I can hardly see straight!" Aniedi started jumping up and down.

"Did you get something in the mail?" Onja raised her eyebrows and smiled, affected by Aniedi's excitement.

"No. Even better. Remember how I wanted you to introduce me to some old-timers?"

"Yes." Onja's voice dipped and returned.

"Well, the big shots on the dig want someone to collect oral history of the valley. I told you I want to hear people stories…now it's really going to happen! Roy or Verna must have told them I would be perfect. And I am perfect! No more digging in the dirt! They're even giving me a budget to buy recording equipment, tapes, everything!"

Onja kept smiling.

Aniedi continued, "I'm driving to Regina today to shop for my equipment. I'll stay overnight at my brother's and drive back Sunday afternoon. So, when can I pick you up for my tour?"

Onja frowned. "What?"

"Pick you up, silly girl. You're my informant."

"Your what?"

Aniedi howled. "I guess informant has some negative connotations. In ethnography, that's a style of anthropological study, the researcher, that's *moi*, needs someone to help her understand the observations she makes about the community she tries to immerse herself in. You'll be my guide, my interpreter…my informant."

"You want me?" Onja poked herself in the chest. "Are you sure?"

"Absolutely. You're young, you won't get in the way, and I'll have someone with me who can make sure I don't get lost. Plus, the old-timers like kids. One of my professors said that. It gives them a reason to talk to you if you remind them it's all about the future. Sorry, but I guess I'm using you."

Onja smiled tightly.

"How about Monday morning, around nine o'clock? I'll be back from Regina late Sunday. Do you think your dad would let me interview him first? And then maybe you could get me hooked up with your uncle West?"

"Dad's in the hardware aisles inside." Onja turned her head toward the Co-op. "We could ask him as soon as I mail this letter."

Onja put the letter on the counter and asked the postmistress if she could see the latest stamps. The elderly woman was as timid as a doe before hunting season, Onja thought. A poster of the John Macoun seventeen-cent stamp hung on the side wall. Seventeen cents, Onja thought. So cheap! That must have been a long time ago.

She considered the old guy in the frame. He looked like a botanist, Onja thought, with his bushy white beard and cattail-fluff eyebrows. His face was superimposed on a landscape picture of himself in a field, notebook under pen. Wouldn't it be fun to be right there with him in the picture? In her valley...

Onja turned back to Aniedi, but she was gone.

The postmistress returned and Onja chose a stamp with tulips on it. Not much better than the queen, Onja teased herself.

"How's young Stacy?" the postmistress asked in her quiet way.

"She really likes Medicine Hat, but she told me to say *hi* to everyone, so she must miss us too."

"Is she making new friends?"

"Yes...she is." Onja tasted the words. They were molding grapes. Sweet at first, then so sour that you have to spit what's left into your hand. "Thank you," she said and turned to the metal rows of mailboxes. Nothing from Stacy, again.

"Goodbye," called the postmistress as Onja left without making eye contact again.

She sat alone in the truck. I'll bet Stacy's wearing makeup now. Probably has her hair cut in the latest style, whatever that is. She's likely joined the fencing club.

Aniedi popped her head into the open window. "Hey, I thought you'd be happy. Isn't everyone happy today?"

Onja faked a smile.

"Lighten up, kid. Whatever it is, it isn't that bad."

Onja's attitude warmed in Aniedi's sunshine. "Yeah, you're right," she said.

"That's more like it. See you Monday." Aniedi capered to her car. Look out, Regina, Onja thought. Here comes the sun!

Wayne chuckled as he slid into the truck. "Now that's quite the researcher. She could talk the ear off a cob of corn. She wouldn't let me go until I drew her a map to the farm."

"She's just excited about history, Dad. It's weird, hey? Interested in our valley. Do you think you'll be able to help her? She's really nice."

Her father's eyes lit up. "Well, there's Blondeau for sure, and your uncle West, of course. And Steinkie, Stregger, Frijoff, Boyer, Gillies, Besplug, Johnson, Blackburn, Muirhead…there's lots of them. Look in the history book when we get home. That'll have all the names."

They rode home, Wayne driving slowly, looking at the crops and talking to himself: "That's ripening nicely…still could use rain. They planted too late and it's getting behind. We could still use a shower before it gets really hot."

He reached over and turned up the volume on the radio. "What was that?"

The radio announcer continued, "You can expect more record breaking temperatures, and no clouds in sight."

Every week the *Noon Edition* program on CBC sponsored a contest. This week it was to finish the phrase "It's so hot that…" Someone phoned in and said, "It's so hot, you can make a horse drink, but you can't lead him to water." Onja sniggered.

Water…everything seemed to be about water.

On Saturday Morning

No satellite dish mushroomed from the Claibourns' roof; cable television was a big-city dream. They relied on rabbit ears to regularly pull in two Saskatchewan signals—Yorkton and Regina—but something magical happened on Saturday mornings; if Onja and Leigh got up early enough, they could tune in a clear NBC signal from nearby North Dakota. The earlier they were up, the better the signal. They watched everything on the lineup. Reruns from television's black-and-white days brought *The Black Stallion* at 9:30, but it disappeared like a landmark in a thickening blizzard by 10:00.

Onja remained on the couch in her pajamas, cuddling her pillow. Leigh changed the channel from *Farm News* to a local variety show.

"Just turn it off." Onja put the pillow behind her head and lay on the couch. Should she phone or not? All morning, between cyber wars and rodent rescues, she'd been trying to psyche herself into phoning Mrs. Foster, her former 4-H leader.

Two years ago, Onja had been in the club with Ginger. On Achievement Day, for which Onja had been training endlessly, Wayne had to bribe Ginger with Leigh's pony just to get her into the trailer. And that was the easy part. Once Ginger was out of the trailer at the fairgrounds, she pranced and whinnied continually at the other horses.

In the halter class, Ginger neighed right in Onja's ear and then reared into the air. Onja dropped the reins, and Ginger bolted for the far side of the outdoor arena. Two men from the audience came to help Onja as Ginger raced around the inner railing. Her father hadn't come. Her mother, she knew, would have been as useless in that ring as a rabbit caught in headlights. Humiliated, but secretly relieved, Onja pulled out of the saddle classes in the afternoon.

Just thinking of phoning Mrs. Foster made her face sting, like the strip of raw burn on the back of her neck. How can I ask her to trust me with her horse after that day? Onja slipped lower on the couch.

Still, Onja thought, the fair wasn't a total waste of time. I did get first in the scrapbook category, and Mrs. Foster had written some encouraging words in the cover. My love for horses, my attention to detail. Stuff like that. And if I don't phone, I won't be able to take Etthen riding in the valley…so maybe I can handle a little embarrassment if that's the reward.

Onja sat up and placed her pillow to the side. It's for a good cause, it's for a good cause, she mind-chanted. Mrs. Foster is one of the sweetest women I know. She's probably forgotten all about my 4-H debut. Yeah right. It took six men to load Ginger when it was time to go home. She pictured

Ginger, hooves dug in, refusing to enter the narrow trailer.

Well, here goes nothing, she thought, her finger beside the Fosters' number in the phone book. The phone rang three times before a familiar voice answered. "Hello."

"Hi, Mrs. Foster?"

"Yes?"

"This is Onja Claibourn."

"Oh, Onja. How are you enjoying your holidays?"

Onja's throat felt dry. So far, so good, she thought and gulped before answering. "Great." She paused and scratched her nose. "Did you plant a big garden this year?"

"Not as big as usual; it's been so dry these past few years, and we haven't got the water to irrigate much. And when it does grow, the hoppers get most of it."

"That's what Dad says too…Uh, Mrs. Foster, I have an unusual request." Onja stood up straight, trying to feel and sound grown-up. "Do you think I could borrow one of your horses for a couple of days? I have a friend who I'd like to take for a ride in the valley."

Mrs. Foster was quiet for a short lifetime. Onja held her breath. Finally the woman spoke. "Sorry, Onja, I was just thinking which horse could use the riding, and which horse would get along with Ginger."

Onja's heart triple-beat.

Mrs. Foster continued, "I think you could take Shane's Blaze. Shane's got a summer job in Regina; then it's back to university in the fall. Blaze could use the attention, but I'd like for *you* to ride him, Onja. I don't know if your friend has ridden much, and Blaze will need an experienced hand."

Is she talking about me? "Sure, I can ride Blaze." Onja looked out the kitchen window toward the pasture. A smile grew deep in her chest and then pumped into her veins.

"Will your dad bring a trailer?"

"Mmm, he's pretty busy these days...would it be okay if I rode Ginger to your place and then led her, or Blaze, home?" Onja bit her tongue.

"I don't see why not."

"Can I come tomorrow, after church?" Onja's breathing was short, as if she'd just run up and down the lane.

"Sure, we'll be home. See you then, Onja. Bye-bye."

Wow, Onja thought, Mrs. Foster was as casual as a pair of jeans. She hung up the phone and whooped. Clapping her hands in the air, she danced to the kitchen window.

"What?" yelled Leigh from the basement. "What's going on?"

"Life is good," Onja yelled back. "Life is really good."

Under the Sun

Onja tied Ginger to the hitch of the little tractor.

Her thoughts returned to the refreshment of the basement. She had walked uneasily toward the landing, kicking off her brown leather heels, then stepped down the stairs. First her ankles, then legs and finally her arms and face had felt the breath of coolness: like walking into a lake. She'd lain on her bed, head drooping over the edge toward a stack of books on the floor.

Ginger dropped her muzzle and severed the harvest-yellow grass one mouthful at a time. The mare's eyes were brown with flecks of burlap. All-knowing.

Onja remembered the novel's cover image staring up at her, a close-up of a girl's eyes, nose and upper lip. Globes within globes and a memory splash of lemonade dripping off eyelashes and into the corners of a mouth. In the book, the kids had been riding in a bike-a-thon; it had been hot like this when a storm rolled in. No chance of that today, she thought. The sun dried the recollection and hope.

Onja walked back to the house.

"Mom, do we have lemonade?" she called from the entryway.

There was no answer.

Onja pulled herself up the stairs, runners a tap with each step. She lingered at the top. The dim sheen of the house baited her: *Here, pull up a spot on my couch where the nasty bright orb can't see you.*

She almost lay down on the couch, but an image of Etthen in the saddle woke her imagination: his hair flowing like a coal bed, his shoulders broad like the high branches of an oak tree, legs strong as fieldstone. Now I sound like a page from the Song of Solomon, Onja thought. I guess Harlequin isn't good enough for Sundays.

Like a man-at-arms, she marched into the kitchen toward the freezer. A bottle half filled with ice would substitute for the tart citrus refreshment. Better not tell Aniedi. She smiled at her own little joke as she topped the second half with water and placed it in a cotton bag.

At least it's not plastic, she thought, stepping into the yard. Cotton, the world should be cotton on a day like today.

Ginger looked at the girl once as she tossed the Navajo blanket and then the saddle on her back. She snorted and sucked a giant breath as if to say *Do what you must.*

Onja adjusted the saddle, leaving room at the mare's shoulders. She hooked the left stirrup around the saddle horn, looped the strap into the cinch, and pulled, inching it tighter and tighter. She looped the strap into a knot.

She placed her foot into the left wooden stirrup, now hanging below the mare's belly, and bounced once. The saddle shifted toward her, horn pointing off-kilter.

"Puffing up your tummy, hey?" Onja scolded. She hooked the stirrup onto the horn again and tightened the strap.

This time Onja was able to land in the saddle after three gentle hops and a swing of her right leg. She adjusted her seat. This thing is as soft as a wooden church pew, she complained to herself. She remembered the day Grandpa brought it to the farm, fresh from an auction sale. It's a good thing it has sentimental value, Onja thought, because it sure isn't comfortable.

By the time she reached the end of the lane the saddle was wobbling from side to side. Onja had seen people knee their horses to discourage them from ballooning their stomachs, but she calmly dismounted and readjusted the cinch.

A whiff of wind was enough to cool the perspiration on Onja's face. She stood in the stirrups. Bare leg against warm horseflesh would not be pleasant today, she thought, conceding gratitude for this cracked saddle.

The unpaved road that stretched two miles north was alive and growling beneath the horse's unshod hooves. Onja reined her mare into the ditch, lined with small square bales. Like park benches on a nature hike, she mused. This second growth of wild grasses were mid-hock on Ginger's leg. If it rained, they might give another crop, Onja thought.

Onja closed her eyes but couldn't escape the clear sky and fireball sun. When you want blue sky, you get clouds; when you want the relief of clouds, nothing but scorching sun. It was like that Joni Mitchell song her mom was always singing: "Don't it always seem to go, that you don't know what you've got till it's gone."

She relaxed her hold on the reins and Ginger gravitated toward the road.

This pattern, in and out of the ditch, continued for two miles until horse and girl turned east for the one-mile ride to the oiled road. Onja gave up and let Ginger walk on the gravel. After all, Onja thought, they're your feet.

Onja relished a new view of her prairie from the road; she usually rode along the low prairie trail. The Pool elevator in Palliser seemed close; she could already see the grove of trees lining Fosters' lane.

This was riding, rather than *being* the prairie, she thought. It looked drier from up here. Everything was *no longer*: the flax was no longer blue, the mustard no longer yellow.

Back in her room, Onja had stared at the book jacket leaning against the other books beside her bed. A giant green butterfly masked a man's green head, both imposing their presence over a brown prairie landscape and brown farmhouse. Brown, the enemy of the prairie. Green, the savior.

Sylvia had brought the novel home from one of her University Women's Club meetings, raving that the author was the next generation of W.O. Mitchell and Sinclair Ross. Another Saskatchewan success story.

Onja had reached down and picked up the novel. Images—a spider squashed on the thirsty earth, the dominant sun, the eternal dust—all remembered at once.

She had flopped backward onto the bed, letting the novel fall to the floor. She had missed her pillow and her head had rolled to the side. She'd stared out the window. The sky was a faded blue, bullied, in its own backyard, by the white sun. How could there ever be enough rain to cool the world outside? Couldn't it at least be cloudy, just today? she had thought. Four miles there and four miles back. What was I thinking?

A dip in the road took the Pool elevator from Onja's view; the air grew still.

They passed a white alkali-rimmed slough carpeted in red samphire where hardy mosquitoes joined the journey, humming onto Onja's arms and legs, Ginger's thighs and neck. At first Onja blew and shook the insects, but soon she was swatting and flicking. Ginger's tail whipped from side to side. Onja wiped Ginger's neck, leaving smudges of blood and mosquito remains on the smooth copper hair.

The almost imperceptible breeze rid the air of their companions as they rode out of the dip.

Onja reached for the water bottle with hot and sticky hands. Ice floated at the top. She took one swig and poured a little onto one hand and then the other, washing the blood while rubbing her legs. She took another splash and bathed her sweat-dried face.

It would sure be nice if there were more water around, Onja thought. The sloughs are dried up, ready for hay. I'd love to jump into a stream right about now.

Onja and Ginger had settled into their rhythm, slogging beneath the sun. There was no need to direct the horse as they turned north again, onto the oiled road, one mile from Fosters'.

The only green was the patch of potatoes coming up on the right of the road, beside a silly-looking dugout with a fence surrounding it and no cattle to drink from its shore. Irrigation pipes lay idle through the lonely garden. These deep dugouts that dotted southern Saskatchewan, Onja had heard Wayne explain, were dug with government subsidies.

Higher than ever, Onja felt a whisper of fear as a dark dot on the road grew. A truck moving toward them. She took the mare into the ditch. Ginger sidestepped, this time fighting the reins to go back onto the blacktop. Onja held the reins tight. The horse rippled with energy. Onja neither looked up nor waved, but held the eight-year-old in as she kicked both back legs with each honk. The vehicle was gone.

"You're just a little girl, aren't you?" Onja said, patting Ginger's neck.

Onja felt the sun less and looked across the road to Fosters' pasture.

Ginger blew out her nostrils and held her neck arched. Too bad you look like a Quarter Horse and act like an Arabian, Onja thought. Ginger let out a blast of a whinny. Onja grabbed for the saddle horn.

"Easy, girl, take it easy." She reached down to pat Ginger's neck.

The horse trumpeted again. Fosters' little herd was running up and down the fence, and Onja pinched the reins, holding Ginger to a walk, keeping the left ditch and black-top between them.

The brilliant chestnut broke into a trot, and Onja let her work out her energy, bringing them closer, faster.

A lone horse stood in the shade of the barn, swatting flies with his black tail. A white blaze shone down his dark brown nose. He turned to watch Onja and Ginger approach the house, his black mane framing the left side of his face: Shane's bay gelding.

Onja felt her shoulders relax. Ginger, too, stopped whinnying and turned to watch Blaze.

"Onja," a friendly voice called from the house. Mrs. Foster. "Come in for some lemonade. You must be baked!"

Onja smiled hello, then grimaced as she stood in the saddle, legs sticking to leather.

"Take Ginger's bridle off and let her into the corral with Blaze. She needs to get out of this sun too," Mrs. Foster instructed.

Ginger's ears bent forward and she snorted as they approached the flag-red barn. Onja dismounted and walked Ginger into the paddock, remembering the red reaction to the "Save-the-Valley" graffiti.

"What's wrong with red these days?" Onja asked the mare. "I thought horses were color-blind."

Ginger, now distracted, trotted toward Blaze like an old friend and scratched his back with her muzzle.

In Fosters' kitchen, with a glass watering in her hand, Onja forgot the sun.

"So what's been keeping you busy?" Mrs. Foster asked.

"Well, first we packed Stacy off to Medicine Hat, and then I went to camp for two weeks…" Onja watched the horses in the corral as darkness passed over the shade from the barn. Shape-shifting cotton and horsetails floated in from the west.

"I hope there's rain in those clouds." Mrs. Foster's voice chanted the prairie mantra.

Onja finished her lemonade.

"Thank you so much for lending me Blaze." Onja took the glass to the sink.

"I'm just glad you asked. He's such a good old soul and I like to see him get a little attention."

They left the house for the barn.

Ten-year-old Blaze was the picture of a color-coordinated gentleman as he walked from the barn, where Mrs. Foster had outfitted him in his black saddle and bridle.

Onja swung into his saddle—which didn't budge, she noted—as Mrs. Foster handed her Ginger's bridle. Ginger followed meekly as a stiff, light wind blew more clouds to shade the ride home.

At the Island

Aniedi phoned at 8:30 on Monday morning. Onja had been ready since 8:00. She wondered if Aniedi had invited Etthen along. There was really no reason, but he seemed to pop up everywhere. Maybe he'd tag along this time too.

Muktuk's bark brought Onja to the door at 8:50. Aniedi pulled into the yard alone. Onja's breath—tight in her gut—leaked through her lips. Guess this is a girls' only adventure, she thought. No love triangle here.

Aniedi was driving a red Firefly. A hand-drawn map lay in the front window dash. She heaved the driver's door open and called, "Onja, will you give me a hand with my stuff?" She's glowing like a child on Christmas morning, Onja thought as she trotted to the hatch of the Firefly. It slowly opened hydraulically, as if the vehicle wanted to increase the drama, revealing a big black bag, a small black bag and a black briefcase. "Wait until I get you inside and show you all this stuff. It's just too cool." She stopped, hand on the small bag. "Is your dad still okay with the interview?"

"Dad's out in the field, swathing hay. He'll want coffee soon."

"That's perfect. I'll have time to set up my equipment. It's top of the line. When those big boys hand it out, they don't spare any expense. If only my friends in Regina could see me now…they'd be green with envy."

Onja took the biggest bag from the car. After all, she thought, I'm the farm girl here. It was almost too heavy for her thin arms, but she was sure not to grimace as she hauled it up the stairs and into the kitchen. "Is the counter okay?" she asked.

"Perfect," Aniedi trilled, setting down the briefcase and smaller black bag. She scanned the kitchen. "Hey, cool, you have an island. Can we sit there?" She pulled out a tall stool, sat down and leaned forward on her elbows and clasped her hands. "We'll gather at the island to talk about the soon-to-be-flooded valley. Get it? Symbolism, I love symbolism."

"Okay." Onja's tone was quiet. The valley would never flood. She looked out the window. A Baltimore oriole, as orange as the Cairo sunset in her mother's pictures, flitted in the dugout trees. She wondered if its chicks were still in their hanging nest or if they were long gone.

By 9:05 Aniedi had turned the kitchen into a recording studio. Onja had to sit still on the stool as Aniedi lined up the video camera on a tripod. A handheld microphone lay on the table—for backup, Aniedi said. She had brought books, *Interviewing Techniques* and *Ethnographer's Field Book*. She tested each gadget and made notes in her scribbler.

Both Aniedi and Onja looked up as Sylvia—dressed in a black short-sleeved sweater and black jeans, what she called her Bohemian uniform—entered the room. Leigh trudged up the stairs behind her, swimming bag in hand.

"You must be Aniedi. I'm Sylvia." She extended her hand. "We've heard a lot about you."

"All good, I hope," Aniedi said.

"Of course. And this is Leigh, the baby of the family."

"Mom," Leigh whined.

They briefly admired the recording equipment, then left for town to spend the morning at the pool.

The murmur of Sylvia's car faded and was replaced by the faint rumbling of a tractor.

"Purrs like a kitten," Onja told Aniedi, who was now sitting at the island. "Dad always says his tractors purr like kittens. I agree…but only when they're far away."

Onja opened the can of coffee and tipped her nose into the rush of aroma. "If only coffee tasted as good as it smells."

"What's wrong with coffee?" Aniedi defended the cattail brown grind.

"Nothing that a half a cup of cream and two scoops of sugar can't fix." Onja rounded a scoop of ground beans and poured it into the white filter.

"That sounds more like cappuccino."

"And you sound like my mom. She says to me, 'That's not coffee,' when I fix it the way I like. When I grow up…" Onja stopped mid-threat.

The door opened. Wayne placed his cap on the edge of the railing, revealing the tan line between his white head and brown face. His four-wheeled, multi-ton kitten roared outside. He clunked downstairs to wash the morning's work from his hands.

"I don't think Dad plans to stay too long for the interview. This is a perfect day for haying." Onja spoke in a confiding whisper.

Aniedi's face dropped and then bounced back into a smile. "That's fine. I've always got a plan *B*."

They heard heavy footsteps on the stairs. Wayne had not taken off his work boots. I hope he's not in too much of a rush, Onja thought. It would be rude and embarrassing.

He poured himself an inky cup of coffee and placed it on the island, then leaned forward on the wooden stool with both hands braced on his thighs. "So, what can I do for you two?"

"Thank you for taking time to speak with me, Mr. Claibourn. I know this is a very busy time of year." Aniedi adjusted the tripod.

"Even farmers need a morning break." He picked up the coffee cup and slurped the beverage. "Please, call me Wayne."

Aniedi turned on the equipment and opened her notebook. "Okay, Wayne. I understand that the MacLeod Ranch belonged to your great-grandmother's people, and more recently to your uncle West. You must have many memories of the valley."

"Sounds like you've done your homework." Wayne smiled at Onja. "Yes, we've got roots down there. And my great-grandpa Claibourn homesteaded the land I'm farming."

"Can you tell me what the valley means to you?"

He paused for a moment and took another drink. "For me, I guess, it's all about history. History of the people. History of the land…" He held the cup up as if he were about to take another sip. "Have you heard about Old Maggot? There's a story that needs telling."

Onja cringed every time she heard her father say the legendary eccentric's name.

"Please, go ahead." Aniedi was all business, but Onja sensed enthusiasm bubbling just beneath her words.

"Well, this old guy, Maggot, was originally from England. Now, which county was it again?" Onja's father jumped up and left the room.

Aniedi left the video and audio tapes rolling and stared at the empty doorway. "Unfortunate name," she whispered to Onja. Onja smiled and nodded.

They heard rummaging and shuffling. "Here it is." He returned with a huge red book: *Settlers of the Prairies*. The book fell open to a page with oil thumbprints in the corner. Wayne pointed at a man sitting cross-legged on a wooden chair with his back to the camera in front of a mound of stones and earth that looked, vaguely, like a house.

"Here's Maggot."

Onja cringed again. Aniedi moved in closer.

"Look here, he was from Oxford County, England. Born in 1858. His claim to fame was that he didn't believe in money. He wouldn't accept money for any work he did, and he wouldn't pay taxes. You know the CPR pump house in the valley? He built that. He was a stonemason, and a mighty fine one at that. Nope, he wouldn't take any money for his work. Folks say that when he finished the pump house, the CPR tried to pay him, but he wouldn't take it, so a neighbor had to collect the money for him and buy what supplies he needed. He really stuck to his principles."

Aniedi's mocha brown eyes were wide and expectant.

"Yup, Maggot was living up in the hills west of Stephan and they threw him in jail. He wouldn't pay his taxes or swear allegiance to the queen. Story goes that one of his neighbors just went into the jail and took him home. So Maggot moved to the correction line, and that's where he lived until he died. He threw up stones and earth. His home looked like a beaver dam rather than a regular house. Rounded like a wigwam."

Onja's father tapped the picture with his pointer finger. "He looks like an English gentleman with a notepad on his lap, legs crossed, like he was consulting with his biographer. That's where the remains of his place still are, right on the correction line, or road allowance. That land is crown land, so he could squat there...*almost* legally. Today he couldn't get away with it, but back then the neighbors all respected him and supported his way of life."

Aniedi nodded. The tape reeled.

"Apparently he was quite a reader, old Maggot. He'd sit there in his chair and read, mostly the Bible, but folks say you could tell he was well-read. And he was completely self-sufficient. He hunted, fished, trapped and hired himself out, and, like I said, he never took a cent for anything. He bartered for everything he couldn't supply for himself.

"They say that one year a weasel bunked in with him for the winter. And he could sing like a bird and even play the piano."

Onja sat still on the stool beside her father. *All the years I've probed the valley, and I didn't know the hermit had built the pump house. I've never seen his shack.*

Her dad paused and took a gulp of the warm coffee.

"Please continue, Wayne," Aniedi prodded.

"You take this book when you go. And you really should talk to my uncle, West Claibourn. He knew the man directly. I've just admired him through the stories. Apparently he was a religious man too. They say he'd preach his message—have his own Sunday services—and teach the kids Bible verses...nobody seemed to mind. He was respected." Wayne whistled. "Wouldn't it have been something to know him?"

The tractor roared as if calling for its master. Wayne jumped up and said, "Now I'd better get back to the hay."

Aniedi concluded, "This has been most informative, Wayne. Thank you for your time." She turned off the camera and recorder. When the door slammed, Aniedi said, "I should have recorded his boots hitting the stairs."

Between Interviews

Onja picked up the telephone and opened a cupboard. Taped to the inside was a handwritten list of names and phone numbers. "Here's Uncle West's number. Dad said we should visit him…no time like the present, right?"

"You're a girl after my own heart," Aniedi said.

Onja dialed while Aniedi stood at her elbow. "Hi, Uncle West. This is Onja."

"Well, how are you, dear? How's that little mare of yours?" Onja held the receiver away from her ear: Uncle West spoke very loudly, and she was sure even Aniedi could hear his baritone voice.

"She's good…we're good." There was an artless pause before Onja continued. "Uncle West, I've met a lady who is doing archaeology in the valley. She wants to meet with you to talk about MacLeod Lake and the valley."

"Really?"

"Do you think she could come see you and Aunt Hazel today? She's asked me to come with her."

"Well, sure…you just bring your friend along and we'll have a good visit and…" He interrupted himself. His voice was momentarily distant and muffled. "Hazel, do you feel like a drive."

"Sure." Aunt Hazel was always up for an event, Onja knew.

"Onja, what do you think about this? Why don't we meet you out on the veranda at the old ranch? There are still some benches and an old swing. That way I can show you around and you'll be able to see what I'm talking about."

"Just a minute, Uncle West." Onja turned to Aniedi and relayed the request, adding, "Do you have batteries? There probably isn't any electricity."

Aniedi opened a compartment of the small black bag to reveal stacks of batteries. "We've got it all!" she mouthed.

"Uncle West? Can we meet you at 1:30?"

"Sure, sure…1:30 on the veranda."

"Perfect…thank you!"

"See you there, dear." He hung up the phone. It was 11:30 AM.

"We have two hours. Do you want to have lunch here?" Onja offered.

"Why don't we go back to the dig site? I'd love to rub everyone's noses in all this. Can you pack yourself a lunch? I didn't cancel mine, so it should be waiting."

Aniedi packed the studio into the three black bags while Onja scrounged through the cupboards. Hope Mom gets groceries in town, she thought. You can only do so much with Sunny Boy cereal.

They lugged the baggage to the car.

Onja opened the passenger-side door and stepped in, holding her brown bag lunch on her knee. "This is way different than the truck," she told Aniedi. "How does it like the gravel roads?"

"It does surprisingly well," Aniedi bragged. "Yup, this little bug and I have put on a lot of kilometers."

They rolled down both windows as Aniedi stepped on the gas, piloting down the lane. "Dust is better than heat," Onja said.

"We're leaving the dust behind," Aniedi corrected.

It felt as if every stone on the lane threw itself at the undercarriage of the car. Onja imagined kayaking over rapids; it couldn't be noisier than this.

They neared Stacy's farm. Onja considered the long lane. How many times had she been driven up and down that runway? Now it was off-limits, yet she wanted to know it more than ever. She speculated: Is there machinery in the yard? Is the porch filled with protection for all seasons: fleeces, wind jackets, vests, parkas, slickers? Which room does he sleep in?

A rock smashed under the car. Onja felt the floor vibrate against her foot.

Is he at the dig?

She looked at her hands. His lips met my skin right here, she thought, touching the opaline skin just below her knuckles. She wove her fingers together. Here's the church. Here's the steeple. Open the door. Where are the people? Her finger congregation regrouped. This time, the people showed.

A flash of yellow bloomed in the ditch. Brown-eyed Susans grinned, their faces popping out of sun-kissed manes. She imagined plucking the petals. He loves me, he loves me not.

She jumped out at the gate and opened it. Aniedi drove through. Onja closed the gate with a heave, slip and yank and jogged to the Firefly.

"I should have been watching how you did that. It takes me half an hour to close that gate. Opening it's not so bad. I just wiggle off that loop of wire and it all falls down." Aniedi stepped on the accelerator and spun out.

The Firefly climbed up one rock and down another. The ultimate speed-bump challenge, Onja thought.

Aniedi stopped the car at the top of the valley.

If I was riding Ginger, I would have stopped right here too, Onja thought. What a view.

"What a view," Aniedi said.

Onja looked at her…Jinx! she thought.

"So your Uncle West lived below MacLeod Park, right?"

"How do you know that?"

"Oh, we've all heard of West Claibourn. He has quite a reputation."

What's that mean, Onja wondered.

Aniedi rolled down her window and rested her elbow on the edge. "Onja, how do you feel about the changes in the valley?" Her voice was direct and gentle, like a kindergarten teacher's.

"I don't feel anything, 'cause nothing's changed." Onja looked out her window at the prairie. A tuft of buffalo grass shimmied in the faint breeze. The golden heads, two on each stalk, batted like false eyelashes.

Aniedi tightened her lips.

Again, on the gravel, it was too noisy to talk.

Aniedi followed the winding path into the valley and then drove even more slowly across the flat covered in huge round hay bales. When they arrived at the main dig, Aniedi was quick to leave the Firefly to run and find her friends. Onja stayed put, opening the car door to let a breeze lick the sweat on her forehead, arms and legs. She closed her eyes. Sunlight pulsed on her inner lids.

Would the water come all at once, like a flash flood? Not likely. Would they let the water from the Little Mouse collect? That would be like filling an outdoor Olympic pool with a straw. Evaporation would get it all. Onja opened her eyes and looked across the flat from valley wall to valley wall. Once she'd seen the valley flood so that it covered the wooden planks of the bridge, but it had dried up in a couple of weeks, leaving brown and wilting river reeds on fence posts and barbed wire.

How could a bunch of scientists or geologists, geographers, engineers, or whoever they are, be so dumb? Look at this desert. Look at that trickle of a river. Nature made this valley this way. What place did man have going and making dams? What a waste. What a big fat waste.

"A penny for your thoughts." Etthen leaned in the window from the driver's side.

Onja sighed. "Hi." She gazed past him.

"Whoa, where are you?"

"I'm here. I'm in this big dry valley." She examined Etthen. Could he catch what she was really saying?

"You'd better come under the tarp before your sunstroke gets any worse. Look at you, sitting there without even your Kaffiyeh to protect you."

Onja realized she was unaffected, even natural in Etthen's presence. She liked it, but she could feel her ease slipping away. She opened the door of the car and got out, smiling a little foolishly. "You must think I'm pretty weird, eh?"

"Weird is good. Weird is good," Etthen repeated.

Onja scanned him and then searched for the others.

"We're all down by the river. You should come and see what Mom found…"

"Etthen," Onja spoke before all her boldness eroded, "I've got a neighbor's horse at my place. Do you want to go riding tomorrow?"

"Sure." He cracked his knuckle.

"Okay, great," Onja said in a carefully understated tone. She peered over Etthen's shoulder, unprepared now to meet his eyes.

"Fill me in on the details later. You've gotta come see what we found."

Around the Awl

The team was huddled around a woman with long, dark braids protruding from a white ball cap. Etthen's mom, Onja surmised, in the center like a quarterback.

"Make way, make way," Etthen called melodramatically. The team parted. Onja joined the circle, next to the play-maker.

"The First People in this valley were great traders," the woman was explaining. "This may have been manufactured in the Lake Superior region. Maybe even *before* fur trading days. One thing's certain: it wasn't made around here."

Celine Mercredi's copper hands cradled an ancient tool.

It looks like an awl, Onja thought, remembering last summer when the shoe repair store reworked the stitching on Ginger's bridle.

The treasure, made of copper, curved like a small, flattened rib bone and tapered to a point for poking holes. It was purple-black between clumps of clay and dirt. Spearmint green, like the Montreal rooftops in the postcard from Auntie Rose, rimmed the edges.

"The La Verendryes' 1734 Map included the Little Mouse on the trade route nicknamed 'The Warriors Trail.'

These First Nation channels were utilized extensively by the fur trade." She raised her head and whispered, like a mother holding a sleeping baby, "Do you want to hold it?" She elevated the prize toward Onja.

Onja cupped her hands. The little object rested in her palms. It's no heavier than a pencil, she thought. "How old is it?"

"If we'd found some more solid evidence, like a carbon-datable, something found in juxtaposition with it, then I might be able to give you a date. Maybe it came to us from the Old Copper Culture, which was located in what is now Ontario and Minnesota. They were masters in their element…using copper for everything from jewelry to hunting tools. If it is Old Copper Culture it could be somewhere between three thousand and five thousand years old…give or take a few centuries."

"Wow," Onja said.

Etthen's mom smiled and looped a stray lock behind her ear. "Copper spear points and crescents have presented themselves in southern Manitoba, and to a lesser extent in Saskatchewan. I was on a dig near Saskatoon when one of the volunteers found a copper spear point. And there was one crescent discovered in Castor Creek in central Alberta not that long ago."

It's like being in the middle of a documentary, Onja thought. Ms. Mercredi was the disembodied narrator. Haunting. All-knowing. Lyrical.

Celine continued, "We know there was extensive trade, but the exciting question is this: Did the people of the Copper Culture migrate west with their technology?" She looked from face to face.

Onja's hands grew stiff with each word. She could no sooner have dropped the trophy than she could have willed rain from the sunshine.

"Even in the heyday of their expertise, their copper works remained fairly simple: just hot or cold hammering the raw ore into shape. We have no evidence that they worked mixed metals. No alloys." She looked up the valley. Eastward.

"If only it could talk." Onja shifted her weight.

"But it can…it will tell us its story when we ask the right questions. Yes, this will be my find of the dig."

"We'd better bag it." Roy produced the plastic that would now protect the artifact.

Onja lifted her pouched hands to Roy. "No, this is Celine's find," he said.

She turned sideways and Etthen's mom took the awl from Onja with her finger and thumb, as if it were a surgical instrument.

A vibration of deliverance shook Onja. She had just held history in her hands. Someone had fashioned the tool. Used it. Carried it from one place to another and mourned its loss. An old woman, or maybe a girl? Onja compassed the valley, east and west. Heat shaking off rock, brush, tree, river seemed to be the ghosts of the valley people.

Etthen's mom placed the awl into her other palm. "Okay, but you know how much I hate this part."

"You'll get back to it this winter when you're in the follow-up lab." Roy's voice was like an uncle's comfort.

The huddle had begun to break up. Onja watched Ms. Mercredi process the artifact: label, bag, store. Aniedi bounced from friend to friend, spreading her own good news.

Onja inspected the site. Where was the guy in the Oilers cap? Jones. He hadn't been with the team around the awl.

"Mom has a new job. A promotion." Etthen squatted to examine a slight plant with salmon blush petals.

"I think those are called buffalo bills," Onja said. She scrunched beside him. "What do you mean, a new job?"

"They've asked her to stay on here throughout the fall and winter. She'll work in Stephan, at the museum. That's what Roy was referring to."

"No way," Onja gushed. "My mom works there part-time." She picked a round rose hip, red as a fireplace, and nibbled on the vitamin-C–loaded skin. The taste was neither good nor bad. It just was. Like the ending of a story. By the time you got there, you knew this was the way it was supposed to be.

"Mom thought this might happen, that's why we brought all our stuff. I guess I'll even go to school at the Comprehensive in Stephan."

Onja's mind was a starless night. *I'll go to school at the Comp.* A firefly thought danced in the darkness. *In Stephan.* A second firefly. A swarm of fireflies. She envisioned long bus rides to school. Maybe sharing a backseat. Her head on his shoulder…

"Etthen." His mother's voice owned the name. "Etthen, aren't you going to introduce me to your friend?"

"Come on, Mom, you know this is Onja." He stood.

Onja picked another rose hip and stretched upward.

"Onja, this nosy woman is my mother."

"I kinda guessed that." Onja fumbled with the berry. "Not the nosy part..."

"Hi, Onja." Celine smiled and extended her hand. "I met your mom and sister the other day."

Onja grinned. "My mom loved your hair."

"Thank you," Celine said, "but it's not too glamorous right now." She tossed a braid behind her shoulder.

Onja's eyes dropped, heading for the prairie. A black T-shirt stopped them mid-fall. Ms. Mercredi's T-shirt said *Etthen* in green print. Onja stared.

"Do you like my shirt?" Celine stretched the cotton, smoothing out the print and picture.

Onja accepted the invitation to look again. It was a circular crest, the heads of a caribou and wolf poised at the top of either side. Within the circle an eagle carried a fish against a shoreline of evergreens. There was a huge sun—or is that a moon? Onja wondered. Snowshoes crossed at the bottom. Above the crest was printed *Etthen*. Below was *Athletics*. Four or five hoofprints walked across the T-shirt.

Onja was aware of her smile.

"Etthen is Dene for caribou." His mother made a fist and tapped under his chin.

Dene? They're from the far north, Onja thought.

Celine continued, "But when he wakes up, I call him Sasazi...Little Bear."

Etthen blushed.

Sasazi. Yes, I like the sound of that, Onja thought. She risked eye contact with the young man, who seemed closer to her age than ever. His eyes pleaded with his mother. Onja imagined he was demanding *No more information*. She rolled his given name on her silent tongue. Etthen. She tasted the idea of caribou. Was it salty or dry? Tender or tough? Dense or stringy?

Onja nibbled on the rose hip.

"Do you know what that was used for?" Ms. Mercredi nodded at the fruit.

"Was it mixed with meat to make pemmican?" Onja said.

"Not if something sweeter could be found. But yes, it staves off scurvy."

"Would you two speak English, *please*?" Etthen scoffed.

Onja chuckled and considered Celine's face. Eyes like navy blue ravens. Cheekbones like Egyptian architecture. Lips like Nefertiti's bow.

On the Veranda

Etthen's not-yet-a-man face and antlered name carved themselves into Onja's heart. When they were with his mother, Onja had seen something that his jean jacket had hidden. A tender glance. A little-boy pout. An awe-shucks kick at the dirt.

The red car flew out of the valley. Why didn't he come with them? Aniedi had offered.

The young cultural anthropologist was watching the fields pass. Onja was glad for the quiet. She stared with dry eyes and a lump in her throat as they passed MacLeod Park. It still seemed as if it had sprouted overnight, like a mushroom. Her grandpa used to pick the meaty fungus from the prairie, and her mother would fry them in butter. Delicious, Onja remembered. But I can't pick mushrooms. Can't tell the poisonous from the non-poisonous.

They snaked down the valley wall until Aniedi stopped at the bottom. "Better not mess with Roy and Verna's latest site," Aniedi warned as they left the Firefly on the trail.

They carried three black bags containing Aniedi's recording equipment past little buildings toward Uncle West, who was leaning over his parked Oldsmobile near his boarded-up house. He wore a cowboy shirt—with red and white stripes—tucked into blue jeans. His white Stetson shaded his face. He looks like a patchwork American flag, Onja thought, red, white and blue.

Aunt Hazel waved enthusiastically from inside the car. They must have the air-conditioning running, Onja thought. Her great-aunt sprang from the Olds wearing a long denim skirt and puffy pink blouse. She trotted her five-foot frame toward them like a miniature pony. You'd never think she was over eighty years old, Onja thought, and I'll bet she's wearing high heels. Hazel's shoes were hidden by the mid-calf grass.

"Give your auntie a big hug." Her voice was like jelly-beans falling from a quarter dispenser, Onja thought.

"Hi, Aunt Hazel." She's wearing makeup, Onja noticed. And her shoes are three inches of pure pink. Always a fashion statement, Onja thought. "Aunt Hazel, this is Aniedi. She's working on the history of the valley."

"Hi, Aniedi. Welcome to our humble abode."

"Pleased to meet you, Mrs. Claibourn."

"Just call me Hazel, dear. Hazel is fine."

A map was spread on the hood of the car. Uncle West was pointing at a line.

"West, aren't you going to say hello to the girls?" Aunt Hazel asked.

He turned his neck, a crooked Claibourn smile warming his face. "Onja. Well, isn't this fun. Give your old uncle a squeeze." After the hug, Onja introduced Aniedi, who then began setting up her equipment on the veranda.

Uncle West whispered to Onja, "What's your friend's name again?"

"An—yed—ee." Onja emphasized each syllable.

"An—eed—dee," West called, "does any of your equipment travel?"

"Of course." Aniedi strapped the camera to her shoulder and held a small tape recorder in her other hand.

At the Olds, Uncle West pointed at the unfolded map. "There are two ravines that run parallel to each other. We'll build a dam here."

We'll build? Onja mouthed the words. Uncle West is *them?* I thought it was just the government making these plans. People who don't know the valley.

West continued, his voice animated, "This is the development that we visualized at one time. This is all subdivisions, you see." He pointed at the two-dimensional fields at the top of the valley.

"It would be beautiful to live along there," Aniedi said.

"Cottages, the very thing. And a boat launch over here. A picnic area. Put trout in here, you know."

"So this is MacLeod Park?" Aniedi leaned with the video camera to get a close-up of the map.

"Yes, MacLeod Park. My grandparents ranched below." His finger tapped the map, the metal hood of the car acting as an amplifier.

They didn't live on the map, Onja thought. Why don't you look across the river? Could you look at your roots face-to-face and still talk about a dam?

West continued, "We've balsam poplar in here. Hazel likes the snappy sound their leaves make."

"What other types of trees are you planting?" Aniedi slowly panned the valley floor.

"Ash, aspen poplar, Russian olive and chokecherry and, uh, what the heck are those other ones? Shrubs, more or less…"

"Buckthorn?" Onja piped in. Her father had made her collect sea buckthorn seeds to sell to the PFRA in Indian Head. They were worth their weight in gold, bringing in over a thousand dollars.

At least they're not planting caraganas, Onja thought. Prairie weeds. But why do I care? All this development for a dead-end dream.

"Yeah, buckthorn and buffalo berry. And then we got some pine, but the darn pines." He removed a hankie from his pocket and took off his hat, dabbing his forehead. "It's too darn hot."

He's got more hair than Dad, Onja thought mischievously. Maybe he has a toupee.

"What's wrong with the pines? They don't take?" Aniedi offered.

"No, they take…but the deer nibble the new growth. Still, some of them are coming because we're watering them now. Onja's dad helped. We got some plastic pipe from the mine and installed an irrigation system."

Dad? So Dad's in on this part too? What would Grandpa think?

West pulled away from the map and stood to his full height. He scoped the hills, the park, the valley wall, the river...like a buck sensing his territory. "If the government had just gone along with us and put the boat launch in here instead of where it is..."

"Why didn't they?" Aniedi backed up and directed the camera fully on West.

"Well, I tell you, the whole thing is political." He rubbed the side of his jaw as if he had a toothache.

Hazel fussed with her skirt belt, blouse buttons, hair clips, and glanced at her husband.

"What do you mean, 'political'?" Aniedi coaxed.

West folded the map abruptly. "Uh...you don't want to hear all that...it's water under the bridge. So, what the heck, you go with the times. You do what you can."

The whole thing's political. Onja tasted her uncle's sour words. Maybe that's what Judas thought when he threw the silver coins back at the high priests.

West threw the map into the backseat of his vehicle. "Let's go for that tour I promised."

"It's about time," Aunt Hazel said.

"Good, good." Aniedi's cheerleader enthusiasm was almost cartoonish, Onja thought.

They followed Uncle West down the hill. A patch of brown cornflower grew in an unbroken spot of prairie. Each flower's center was a small rocket, and its orangey red petals trailed behind like a fiery jet.

"Right. So, where's this road lead?" Aniedi asked as she caught up to Uncle West.

"It follows the lake and then out of the valley to Palliser. We had to build on this side of the river so the kids could get to school," Uncle West said, walking stiffly.

Aniedi whistled. "It's gorgeous."

"This was our bank barn." He pointed to the side of a hill. He and Aniedi walked ahead. Onja and Aunt Hazel followed.

"A what kind of barn?"

"A bank, you know."

"Oh, you built it in the side of a hill."

"Yeah…we had about three hundred acres in the valley for hay. The rest was pasture…it was good." He spoke in a lilting melancholy, as if in thanksgiving for former blessings.

He continued, "This is the river, of course." He pointed toward the bank, where silver burweed and arrow grass grew among the cattails. Aniedi followed his words with the camera.

He gestured up to the yard. "That's a granary. That's an elevator office we moved from Palliser. It's a great place for storage."

Onja looked at the hazy-day gray of the old buildings. You mean, that *was* a granary and that *was* an elevator, Onja silently corrected the tense of her great-uncle.

She considered West Claibourn. His gaze was far off. Is he remembering war or drought or what he had for lunch? Onja wondered. She turned toward the dilapidated buildings and slapped on imaginary paint: white with black trim for the granary; the elevator white and green. For a moment she wondered if she was now looking through Uncle West's eyes.

He led the tour to the opposite side of the shacks. "And we even had a bunk here when we had the Indians working for us."

Onja cringed when West said *Indians*. There was nothing mean in his voice, but if he'd said servants, or slaves, he wouldn't have needed to change his tone. I wonder if he's ever thought of them as First People? Or that they were the first nations in this country?

West continued, "That was the shop at the back. This was a partition where the office was." The windows were empty, like a boxer with his teeth knocked out, Onja thought.

"A little bunkhouse?" Aniedi asked in the moment he paused.

"Yeah, it worked good. Of course, these are the big sheds. I bought the barn for a thousand dollars. It was a hundred and ten feet long, so we cut it in half before we moved it."

Aniedi's jaw dropped. "Now that's recycling."

"It worked perfect for us."

Onja compared the ramshackle buildings. None of them matched, but Uncle West's so proud, she thought.

They neared a pole fence in varying degrees of decay. "Of course, these are our corrals. One for cattle, another for calves. This one had water in it." West leaned on the corral post with both his elbows.

"Water from the river?" Aniedi tripped over a fallen pole, but quickly recovered her balance. She framed West Claibourn's profile against the log post and valley backdrop. Picture-perfect, Onja thought.

"No, from the well." Uncle West faced the camera. "We had water piped all over the darn place. Anyway, everything was really working good, except we had no control over Mother Nature. The water would flood and then it would get dry. They ruined the valley with the drainage."

"Who is 'they'?" Aniedi asked.

"Farmers got together upriver and ditched the marsh. Five hundred thousand acres of marsh. They drained it and farmed it. They had all these trenches and what they called the thirty-five–mile ditch, and then all the lateral ditches." Uncle West's eyes gazed upriver. He's traveling into the past, Onja thought.

"What impact did this have on your ranch?"

She sounds like a pro, Onja thought.

"If it rained three or four inches upriver, in about four or five days we'd be flooded out because there was nothing to stop it between there and our place." He pointed upriver.

"Because the meadow was gone?" Aniedi said.

"Yes, and sloughs and every nook and cranny that needs the water along the way."

"When did the ditching start?" Aniedi held the microphone a little closer to her subject.

"Early nineteen hundreds, but not so intensive. In about fifty-three we got, what? About twenty inches of rain in June, and it flooded all that up there…" He pointed to a nearby hay meadow. "And those guys living close to Regina were just in there getting ditches…ditching and flooding other guys. Oh, it was bad."

"That's not too neighborly," Aniedi judged.

"No, but I guess it's hard to blame them. They were just trying to do the best by their own families."

Aunt Hazel had wandered from the group, picking a bouquet. Woody prairie sage and delicate pasture sage accentuated yellow buttercups and pink asters. When I get married, Onja thought, I'll carry a handful of flowers from this valley.

Uncle West continued, "Bridges were washing out…it was just a heck of a mess."

"So anybody down the line…" Aniedi began.

Uncle West interrupted. "The trouble here is, once it got down in our area, the elevation drops about an inch to the mile. Well, it's almost as flat as a floor. So once you've got the water, there's no way for it to get away."

Onja shook the cross pole of the fence. It's pretty stable, she concluded, as she climbed to the top and sat on the round railing. She absorbed the valley from her perch. Blue green and beige brown grasses waved, shuddered, whispered everywhere: brome, timothy, reed canary, wild rye.

Aniedi said, "The water would just go off into the…"

"Meadows, yeah. So it put us out of business. And maybe the next year it was dry. Yup, once they started draining, then you had no control."

Aunt Hazel added tall white yarrow to her collection. She grew up in the Qu'Appelle Valley, Onja remembered. I bet she did that when she was a little girl.

"How high was the river?" Aniedi asked.

"It didn't have to get that high to flood the whole valley. We thought we'd build dykes to at least save the meadows, but the water went right over them."

"That must have been something."

"It was so terrible." He shook his head. "You could see it coming. All of a sudden it was over the dyke." His hand leapt like a buck over a fence.

"Onja," Aunt Hazel called, "I want to show you where I kept my garden."

Onja jumped down into the thick growth. With each step she laid the grass sideways, making the ground bouncy beneath her runners. She'd learned this trick walking barefoot on the prairie.

They wandered back, past the house and down a dip. They waded through tall grasses and stepped into a perennial flower garden lined with oddly shaped round rocks called contusions. One looked like a snowman, Onja thought.

Onja smelled the spice of mini-carnations: cinnamon, like Etthen, she thought.

"Go ahead, pick some to take home. They're not doing anyone any good down here."

Onja reached to snap a daisy, but she hesitated. "No," she said, "they're perfect just the way they are."

Against the Pump House

"That should be good," Onja said as she stuffed her backpack with picnic food.

"It sure should be," her dad said, startling her." Where are you off to?"

"Down to the river," she answered, feeling a warmth climb from her neck to her cheeks.

"That's a pretty big lunch for one." His lips were smug, she thought, like a kangaroo court judge. He knows why I have Shane's gelding.

"Dad, it's nothing. Just a ride in the valley." Onja went back to the cupboard and dug for serviettes.

"Your mom and I used to go on picnics too…" He chuckled and left the kitchen.

It's nothing like that, Onja thought as she tucked red poinsettia serviettes into her backpack.

She brought the saddles up the stairs and onto the landing one at a time.

Ginger and Blaze whinnied as Onja waved the white bucket. She kept the bridles behind her back. They trotted across the pasture, Ginger bucking a little as she broke into a canter.

Onja brought the horses to the garage. Ginger puffed out her belly as Onja brought the girth up to the cinch. "Why can't you be more like Blaze?" Onja said as she gave Ginger a little knee in the belly so she could tighten the cinch.

The prairie trail south of the farm was dry and packed hard from a hot summer. Onja rode Ginger and led Blaze, their hooves clopping in time and then out.

She didn't feel like hurrying and neither did Ginger. The plan had been to meet Etthen at the pump house at noon—he was cycling there—have some lunch, then go for a ride. She should have insisted on riding to his place, but he wanted it this way. It was now only midmorning.

The ditches were cut for hay, leaving a sweet smell. Soon she and her father would bring in the bales. Usually she drove the truck, while Thomas and Wayne threw the bales into the back. Maybe this year Leigh will drive and I'll throw with Dad, she thought.

The fields were golden with wheat. The canola crops had lost their yellow flowers. The flax, which had been so beautifully blue to Onja's eyes, was now a gray black as it grew closer to harvest time. Onja had helped her father by driving combine last summer, but more often she was in charge of bringing meals out to the field. There was nothing better on a hot summer evening in the field—with the grain dust floating in the air and the sun setting—than eating corn on the cob and water-melon, drinking brewed ice tea and swinging her legs off the tailgate of the truck, Onja thought.

Onja dismounted at the Texas gate, opened the wire fence to the side and led both horses through.

Ginger sidestepped, keeping the most distance possible between herself and the downed fence. Onja encouraged, "Good girl." She petted the side of her soft neck. Soon the silky hair would start growing thick for winter.

Onja led the horses rather than climbing back into the saddle. As they came to the top of the valley, a chill wind blew and Onja shivered, despite the sunshine. She looked toward the west to make eye contact with the hollow windows of the pump house, but what caught her eye was a bright orange machine with huge wheels, just to the right of the old building.

She swung into the saddle and urged Ginger into a quick walk, Blaze following. When they reached the valley floor, Onja took a handful of Ginger's mane with her right fist and pushed her into a slow gallop. Blaze kept stride. The whole time her eyes latched onto the fire-orange machine beside the pump house.

A bulldozer. The small shed to the side of the pump house had been demolished, and now the driverless contraption was poised—ready with one push—to knock in the walls of her fieldstone castle.

She dismounted and looped the horses' reins onto the pole of a wooden fence. She sat in the hollow stone window with the lunch pack still on her back, staring at the monster.

She heard the rustling of feet in the dry grass. Etthen did not say anything as he walked up beside her.

Onja's eyes gaped like the window she sat in. *Who could do such a thing?* Her head throbbed, just like the first time she'd met Etthen.

He joined her in the window, as if together they might will the orange beast away. The machine dozed in the summer sunshine, and Onja's stomach growled.

She turned to her silent friend. "Are you hungry?"

"Sounds like *you* are." He elbowed her in the side as her stomach rumbled again.

Onja's eyes followed her heart back to the menacing bulldozer. "What's going on here?" she finally asked.

Etthen took the knapsack off her back and jumped down from the shaded window. He walked to the back of the pump house, and Onja heard him spread the plaid blanket, which she had tied like a bedroll to the knapsack. She vaulted from the ledge, her ankles shooting with a cold pain, and walked to the back. Etthen had already pulled out the sandwiches and drinks.

"I can't believe they'd knock down this building," Onja said. "This valley will never flood, but they're ruining it just the same. Why can't they leave things alone?"

"Doesn't make sense to me either."

They sat together, backs against the wall.

Etthen finished his apple. "Let's go for that ride you promised me."

Onja tightened Ginger's cinch, then untied her rein and gave it to Etthen. He stepped into the stirrup and stood straight up before coming down on the saddle.

Onja followed, climbing onto Blaze. The saddle is so soft, Onja thought, distractedly.

"Now, what do I do with these ropes?" Etthen asked.

"Are you serious?"

He laughed. "What…do you think we have these big dogs in the north?"

"Oh. I'd assumed you knew what you were doing. You seemed so…natural."

"Nope, nothing natural about me on a horse."

Onja frowned.

"What, do you think I'm a longhaired Indian in a spaghetti Western or something?" He laughed.

Longhair. Onja recalled her first impression of Etthen. She remembered the black-and-white movies she'd watched with Thomas. Indians were as natural with horses as cowboys were with guns. Maybe he thinks I should know how to fire a six-shooter, and I hate guns. She flushed. Did I really think he was a TV Indian?

"Earth to Onja."

"Oh," she stammered. "Well, you just hold them in one hand." She leaned across Blaze and repositioned Ginger's reins in Etthen's hand. "And tighten up a bit, like cinching up on a baseball bat. The snugger you hold, the better control. When you want to go one way, you press the reins against her neck." She demonstrated with Blaze. Etthen tried and Ginger responded.

"Let's move it out," he said, nudging his heels into the mare's sides. She jumped forward. Etthen held on to the saddle horn and stabilized himself. "Maybe we should just follow you."

Onja took the lead. "This is Stony Crossing," she said as they approached the dry riverbed that was reinforced with rocks the size of ten-pin bowling balls. "Farmers drive machinery across year-round. It's never deeper than three or four feet."

He considered the crossing. "I see what you mean. How can they flood this whole valley when nature can't even keep this stream going all summer?"

"When I was little I used to ride my bike and meet the Davidson girls. We would swim for hours in this hole to the side of the crossing and then have a contest to see who had the most bloodsuckers leached to her body. I remember pulling off fourteen in one afternoon."

Etthen grimaced. "Now that is really gross!"

"Hey." Onja nipped the reins. Blaze halted and Ginger stopped too, back weight leaning on one leg. Onja pointed ahead at a barbed wire fence. "Montgomery's fence is down."

"Oh no!" He mimicked the alarm in her voice and cupped his free hand over his mouth.

"Montgomery guards this fence like it's an international border. One time, when I was little enough to stand in the cab of the truck, Dad and I ended up on Montgomery's land. He came tearing across the field, dust clouds choking the air…I remember Dad saying, 'Man alive, what's the old coot want now?' I was scared too."

Onja stood in the saddle as if she expected the scene to be reenacted at any moment.

"Montgomery caught up with us and jumped out of his truck yelling and cursing. Dad tried to tell him that, we were driving on the road allowance, which divides every quarter section of land in Saskatchewan, and that, technically, we were driving on provincial land, but Montgomery kept yelling and freaking out. Finally we just drove off, leaving the old man shaking his fist."

"Let's check it out," Etthen dared her, reaching across and slapping Blaze on the rump.

She felt creepy crossing the fallen fence, like entering someone's vacant home.

The horses walked side by side for a long time. The valley continued as usual with gopher holes, cactus balls and prairie wool.

Two sets of ears tipped forward, pointing. It was a vehicle, far off, which sent a tremor down Onja's back.

Onja and Etthen looked at each other and said, "Montgomery!"

She pulled to a stop, prepared to panic. Etthen started to laugh. Onja looked at the hills as if there were lurking bandits. Pictures of the old-timer flashed into her mind.

"What's he going to do? Shoot us?" Etthen laughed some more.

"No, but that doesn't mean I want to get yelled at either," she sulked.

"I hope Montgomery isn't hiding behind that hill with his shotgun," Etthen badgered.

"I think I want to turn back…"

"Look, a deer!" He pointed at a caramel-colored doe leaping on the hill. "Come on, let's follow."

He nudged Ginger into a trot—holding onto the saddle horn with both hands—and tracked the deer up the incline. He stopped at the top. Onja pulled alongside and gasped.

Logs piled like stacked matches. Bush piled and scorched black. Hundreds of stumps dotted the valley floor.

An engine roared and then went silent.

The image of the bulldozer flooded Onja's mind.

Etthen slid off Ginger and walked over to the nearest burnt mound. Onja stayed on Blaze and followed.

She felt like she was at the funeral of a distant relative. She was nostalgic for someone she had met once as a child and would now never have the chance to really know.

Etthen continued winding his way between logs and stumps. Neither spoke over the fallen grove.

They exited the waste.

"I've got to tell Jones about this," Etthen said.

"Where was he? I didn't see him yesterday," Onja said.

"He quit. Couldn't live with himself. So he's pumping gas in Stephan."

Onja nudged Blaze into a canter up another incline and stopped. Etthen trailed on Ginger and jumped off at the top. The mare pawed the ground and pulled on the bit by lifting her head.

Onja swung her leg over Blaze's head and sat sideways. Blaze did not drop his head to graze.

The sun was less direct, indicating around six o'clock, but there were no curfews. Clouds were forming in the west.

Onja dropped to the ground and Etthen sat beside her. She pulled grass blades, looking for a thick one to make a reed between her thumbs. One that would squawk so loud that the ducks would fly for cover.

"Look what the wind blew in," a voice said.

Etthen sprang to his feet and Onja almost turned a somersault.

Under the Clouds

Etthen's mom wore a loose white pirate shirt, a flower-print sun hat and green jeans. A pink toothbrush bristled from her front pocket.

"Mom, are you trying to give us heart attacks?" Etthen pounded on his chest.

And are you trying to cough up a spare lung? Onja wondered.

"What are you doing here?" Etthen asked.

"Just some finishing touches on one of our treasure spots. I went to move the truck and it flooded, so I have to let it sit for a while." She regarded the horses. "Are these yours, Onja?"

"Just the chestnut. The bay is our neighbor's."

"Do you mind if I have a little ride?" She walked toward Ginger.

"Sure, go ahead."

Etthen handed the reins to his mom.

They were only a few hundred yards away from a dig site. Celine rode ahead. She sat tall, her limbs loose.

Etthen and Onja followed on foot. Onja led Blaze.

Celine reined Ginger, facing the valley. "You'd never know, just by looking, that this valley has a long human history. Thousands and thousands of years." She turned to the kids. "Makes our lives seem fairly short, hey?" She glanced back to the river. "I wish we had more time. I know this valley is full of campsites, kill sites, ceremonial sites…and all the recent inhabitants."

"What's that?" Onja pointed at a mound of rocks mixed with sod beside a neat pile of stones. It looked like a little garden tractor had taken a nibble and spat it out.

"That's a burial site. A sloppy backhoe driver unearthed it last week while he was…" Celine nodded at the wasteland below. Her voice was sad but not angry.

Onja remembered her grandpa telling about old Indian graves…First Nations graves. It had not been a pretty sight: bones unearthed, sacred possessions taken. She imagined Celine bending toward the earth, picking up the white remains, unable to keep her professional interest separate from her respect for this ancient person. She must have wanted to keep the articles, maybe even a medicine pouch.

"Did you rebury it, I mean…" Onja stammered.

"No. There are protocols that archaeologists and construction companies are required to follow if a grave is unexpectedly disturbed. As soon as it is discovered, the archaeologist must contact the government, and then contact is made with the closest Aboriginal community. Reburial is done according to their expected customs."

Onja's gaze floated from the burial site. The unit squares look like shallow graves, she thought.

"No one asked permission from this old one's grandchildren," Celine said.

No one asked. Onja considered these words. If someone dug up Claibourn graves in Palliser, it would be a scandal. *Permission?* No one would give permission for something like this.

"Makes me feel like a pawn." Celine's voice was soft.

Ginger made a razzing sound with her muzzle and dropped her head to graze.

Celine's voice regained strength. "The big-game hunters came after the Ice Age, and the transition from glacial conditions to conditions that supported bison lasted from about 10,500 BP to 7800 BP."

"BP?" Onja said.

"BP means before present, present being arbitrarily set as 1950, so that translates into 8500 BC to 5800 BC, the days when they could have hunted great bison, camels and the legendary mammoth."

Onja's eyes wandered the wasteland below.

"The oldest dig in Saskatchewan that I'm aware of is the Heron Eden site near Leader, dated to 7000 BC, which involved *Bison antiquus,* a larger form of bison than today's species. Surface finds of Clovis points may indicate earlier habitation than that, but artifacts need to be found in direct association with bones to confirm this."

The voice soothed Onja. Rather than imagining the future of the valley, she took comfort in its past.

"Around 5700 BC the spear was replaced with atlatl technology."

"With what?" Onja and Etthen chimed.

"Pop jinx," Etthen was quick to say.

"The atlatl was a throwing stick with a hook on the end, used to launch a slender spear with great force and velocity. It enabled the hunter to hunt more effectively than with the hand-thrown or stabbing spear. The so-called spear actually had two parts: a long shaft and a dart—a short piece of wood with a stone point lashed to its end with sinew— inserted in the killing end of the long shaft. The atlatl end had a notch into which the atlatl was inserted." She shifted in the old saddle. "And the increased use of the Oxbow atlatl dart around 2700 BC indicates a stronger human presence in this valley."

"Oxbow?" Onja's voice was a punch of excitement.

"Don't forget you owe me a pop," Etthen interrupted.

Onja crinkled her nose at him.

"Yes, named Oxbow because the original point of that style was first named by archaeologists in the Oxbow Dam Site dig, near the town of Oxbow, not that far from here."

"Cool," Onja said. "We bought Ginger from a farmer outside of Oxbow."

"The Oxbow is often mistaken for an arrowhead; however, it is too large. An arrow would be top-heavy with a three-quarter-inch or larger Oxbow dart point on the end."

"What are the earliest sites being studied in this valley?" Etthen asked.

"About 1200 BC. That little piece of pottery Onja and Aniedi found, judging by its style of decoration, was from around AD 0."

Onja looked into the hills.

"Up over there," Celine pointed to the hills, "there are some tipi rings."

"Yes, I've seen them," Onja said.

Celine resumed her lesson. "By AD 200, the bow and arrow was commonplace. This efficient tool increased the viability of the bison cultures."

Onja had often thought of the first people. Celine's words animated her imagination.

Etthen's mom held her hair back in a ponytail. "Layers of evidence indicate the popularity of these sites until recent times. I could spend my whole life sifting through this valley, but my orders are to wrap it up this summer and have my report ready by next spring."

"Have you already started your report?" Onja asked.

"Just my field notes. I'll be working on this all winter."

Celine's truck came into sight. The sun had dropped lower in the sky and the clouds were darkening. They still had a long ride to the pump house. "Etthen, you and Onja had better start back."

Ginger whinnied and swatted a horsefly with her tail.

"I think your mare wants to go too." Etthen's mom dismounted and handed the reins to Onja. "I'm going home to make supper...a late supper." She strode toward her truck.

Etthen leapt onto Ginger's back. Onja swung into the luxurious Foster saddle. Glad to be riding Blaze, she thought.

The truck revved but didn't turn over. The sound was like an angry child's tantrum, Onja thought. Celine leaned out the window. "Still flooded." A wash of fumes confirmed her diagnosis.

The three looked to each other, the truck, the horses.

"Two could double on Ginger…" Onja's voice lingered on the option.

Etthen and his mom hesitated. Onja waited.

"Onja, could we leave the saddle in the truck? That would make an easier trip for Ginger," Etthen offered.

"I suppose it would be more comfortable for whomever rode on the back," Celine said.

Etthen hopped down. "How do you undo this contraption?"

Onja dismounted, unlooped Ginger's cinch and yanked the saddle into the cab of the vehicle. Ginger shook.

Etthen bounded onto Ginger, almost overshooting the mare's back. "Here, climb aboard," he said to Onja.

I'm going to ride with him and not his mother? Onja felt her lungs fill, as if with helium.

Celine walked toward Blaze and held her hand out for the reins. Onja delivered.

"Come on, Onja." Etthen looked into the sky. "Those clouds don't look so friendly."

"Make a stirrup with your foot, like this." Onja demonstrated a crooked ankle at the end of her straight leg. "Just brace yourself." She stepped onto his foot and swung behind him neatly, immediately dropping her arms by her sides.

Celine rode ahead.

They followed the coulee for about half an hour. Celine shared, her voice just audible. "Even before Europeans arrived in the area, their horses, guns and diseases reached southern Saskatchewan through trading among First Nation groups. These foreign influences forever changed the way of life on the plains…that's how Indian Head got its name. Smallpox skeletons…Indian Head."

Etthen and Onja rode in silence, with Celine punctuating the stillness with her abundant knowledge of local history.

"Europeans built homesteads in the Little Mouse Valley in the late 1800s and early 1900s. Remains of these early historic buildings, such as the cellar depression at the base of this hill, are being studied in the historic archaeology part of the Heritage Study."

A meadowlark called as though a haunted prairie loon.

"And you know, it wasn't just white farmers who made a go up there on the prairie. Some blacks made it across the border, all the way from Oklahoma, already experts in dry-land farming. Aboriginals farmed successfully too…" Celine paused. "Until they were too successful."

Too successful. Celine's words wisped like a soft broom after cobwebs in Onja's mind.

"How could anyone flood this paradise?" Etthen directed his voice backward, for Onja's ears only.

She took a deep breath and her heart felt as though it had wings. It didn't matter what she did or didn't know.

It didn't matter how or why she had arrived here; this moment was worth everything. Someone else loved her valley. And someone seemed to like her.

The sun started setting when they reached the river. Marigold rays gave an eerie aura to lengthening shadows.

The wind picked up and Onja was glad for the backpack. Still, as they rode, the goose bumps from the cooling wind competed with the goose bumps from being so close to Etthen.

Celine rode farther and farther ahead.

The sun retired quickly. "Where did all the clouds come from?" Etthen turned Ginger sideways and nodded at a black front visibly covering the sunset.

"Looks like rain," Onja said.

"Hope it's not snow," Etthen joked.

Just the thought of rain made Onja even chillier. She slid in closer to Etthen.

"Onja…" His voice was like hot chocolate, she thought. "It's okay if you sit closer. I know you're cold."

She nestled in. He grasped her dangling hand and placed it around his stomach. Then the other arm. "This is okay," he whispered.

She made no attempt to disagree or comment, and when the rain came, she buried her face in Etthen's hair and closed her eyes. Her body shivered with cold and newness. Something was changing deep inside; she was not embarrassed and she did not feel foolish. Sensations bolted and lingered: red sunset, screeching eagle, heavy quilt, blue campfire…I wouldn't want to be anywhere else, she thought.

When Ginger stopped in front of the pump house, Onja did not let go of Etthen. Her heart ached knowing that she had to go home.

Celine circled back and yelled into the rain. "I think we should just ride for our place. It's closest."

A thunderclap spooked Ginger and she reared slightly.

"Sure, let's go," Onja agreed.

"I'll pick up my bike later," Etthen said, firming the plan.

They turned their backs to the bulldozer and headed for home.

After the Rain

Onja was awake. Orange and yellow sunspots flared on her inner eyelids. Forgot to close the blinds, she remembered. She rolled away from the light.

The sunbursts darkened. She could see the bulldozer—parked like a tank—ready to fire, she thought.

Had it been twelve hours? The alarm clock shone 9:27. More than twelve, she realized. She closed her eyes.

She imagined the pump-house windows like questioning eyes and the door a gasping mouth.

Her hand scrunched a patch of the denim quilt. She rubbed the rough cotton between fingers and thumb. The yarn tassel tickled her palm.

Her throat recoiled. There was no warning. It was like falling from a tree house, she thought. *How could they do this to her? That historic building? It deserved better.*

She lay on her side. Knees tucked in. Head bent forward. A fourteen-year-old fetus.

Onja wiped her eyes.

A scratch on the door. "Onja." Her mother's whisper was barely audible, a snowflake on a frozen window, Onja thought. It lingered, six-sided and unique. "Would you like some tea?"

Mom's answer for everything, Onja mused. "Sure." Her voice was more pout than she'd anticipated.

"How did you sleep, sweetheart?" Colorful cranes flew across the black tray Sylvia set on the dresser.

"Fine." She tried to remember her dream, something about Montgomery.

"Mom, does old Montgomery still live in the valley?"

"What makes you think of him?"

"I think I had a dream about him." Onja looked to the poster on the ceiling.

"He passed away a few years ago. Your father went to the funeral." She poured tea into Onja's favorite mug—a dun mare and foal on Kentucky bluegrass.

"Do you know they're cutting trees and knocking down buildings in the valley?"

"Has it gone that far?" Her mother fussed with the curtains.

"It's wrong. There is nothing right about it."

Sylvia straightened Onja's dresser: buckskin ceramic horse, trophy, cactus… "Well, dear, life's like that sometimes," she said.

What's that supposed to mean? Onja knew there was nothing that her mother could say to help. No one understood what she was going through, but at least she's trying, Onja reasoned. It's not her fault.

"Thanks for the tea, Mom." She sat up and took the mug in both hands. "Ouch."

"Careful. It's hot," Sylvia warned.

Onja took another sip. The apricot steam soothed like her mother's slowly massaging hand on her ankle.

"Mom." Onja's tone was desperate. "There's nothing anyone can do…the pump house is probably gone by now."

Sylvia sighed. "When I was at university we protested the demolition of the oldest movie theater in Regina, but down it went. And the elevators. I hear Palliser's only landmark might not have many years left." Onja saw her mother's eyes as vintage green, peering out the window.

"Mom." Onja's voice had a hint of a smile. "Mom, come back…hello…"

Sylvia returned to the present.

"That wasn't exactly encouraging." A breath of laughter surged from Onja's nose. "Aren't you supposed to try to cheer me up?"

"You know, Onja," she stopped rubbing her daughter's ankle, "I've been doing some writing, and I've figured something out. I'm calling it 'The Four *L*'s of Life.'"

Onja wished Thomas was there. He'd have some witty thing to say, meaning *Here we go again*.

Sylvia continued, "In every difficult situation you face, there are four things you can do. First, Learn. Every situation has a lesson. Second, Laugh. Maybe not right away, but there will be something to laugh about. Third,

Let Go. You must expel the negative energy. Fourth, Love. There's always someone needing your love."

Love, Onja thought. Maybe there's some*thing* needing my love.

Sylvia tapped her daughter's foot. "Celine Mercredi phoned."

Onja sipped the fruity broth again. "Oh?"

"Some guest archaeologists are visiting, and she's having everyone to her place this evening. Do you want to go?"

"She invited me?" Onja held the ceramic cup to her cheek.

"Maybe it wasn't her idea…" Her mother tickled Onja's arch.

"Mom…" she whined.

"So maybe you can get out of bed before *noon* and help me with some housework."

"Did I say I was going?" She glanced at Superman above.

Her mother pinched Onja's big toe, then walked to the window and cranked the metal handle. A honey clover breeze fanned the curtains and rattled the poster on the ceiling. A memory of rain.

The door clicked shut.

Superman's arms stretched forward, willing his flight. His bulked chest beneath blue nylon was too much fun. Levi jean eyes. The man is a god, Onja thought. Christopher Reeve…even after his accident, he still had *it*. Just like Clark Kent had *it*, glasses and all. Onja was Lois Lane—quirky, distracted, too busy for love—until *he* flew into her life.

Onja pulled the blankets over her head. Warm like a sleeping bag. Familiar as sleep.

Had she really had her arms around Etthen? The Superman theme thundered into her mind. Etthen definitely had *it*.

What did he mean, "This is okay"?

His hair had been Irish Spring fresh—Dove soft—Ivory clean, like shampoo suds against her cold face. Oh great, she thought, here I go into Harlequin mode again. She recalled his stomach ribbed tightly under her arms. Her legs spooned against his.

A sugar pink warmth seeped into her chest, like cherry cough syrup, she thought. Sweet.

I wonder what color I should wear to the party.

At Stacy's

Onja glanced over her shoulder as she stepped up the cement stairs to Stacy's old porch. Sylvia waved from her white Tempo.

Onja bent her wrist and then flicked her hand mouthing, "Shoo."

Sylvia mouthed back, "*Aren't we rude.*"

Onja offered an apologetic smile.

Sylvia grinned and mouthed back, "Okay, okay," and drove away.

White paint with purple trim. Cheerful valances in the windows. Petunias simmered cinnamon and peppermint in the evening heat. The house was the same.

The door opened and a strong smell, like a campfire, had replaced the welcome of Stacy's mother's homemade buns. The porch linoleum was polished, and a bleachy clean scent hung in the air. There were summer coats hanging on the porch wall and a variety of runners on the black mats below. A huge pair of gray longhair mittens hung on braided bright cord like the string mothers put through children's parkas. Who could lose a pair of mitts like those? Onja wondered.

"Those are wolf mitts." Etthen's mom stood to the side of the door.

"Oh, sorry. I…"

"Things must seem different. Etthen told me your friend lived here."

"That's right. Sorry…"

"Come on in. Etthen and Sara are in the basement."

Onja grinned as if she were in a toothpaste commercial. Sara who? she wondered.

"Etthen, Onja's here," Celine called down the stairs.

"Be right up…"

He sounded casual enough, Onja assured herself.

Footpads on the stairs. Two at a time. "Onja. Cool. Can I get you a drink? How about a rye and Coke?"

"Uh…" She looked into the kitchen after his mom.

"Just kidding…this is a dry house. Can I get you a pop?"

"Sure…" she said, adding, "it was good of you to bring the horses home yesterday. Dad said they looked well cared for."

"Not a problem." He bounded away.

She smoothed her jeans and then touched her bare shoulder. She'd gone with a sleeveless black sweater. Now she wasn't sure it was the right decision.

Etthen slid across the floor and knocked against her feet. "Sara's in the basement!"

"Great." She faked the enthusiasm. Am I supposed to know her? she thought as she went down the stairs.

A young woman with curly, pumpkin orange hair sat on the couch. "Hey, Cuz." She waved.

"Pardon me?" Onja stared at the friendly stranger.

"Don't you remember me?"

Onja studied the girl's face. She had thin, ruddy lips bent into a crooked smile. Ceramic skin. Spunky round eyes. Sure, she could be Etthen's girlfriend, Onja thought.

The redhead spoke confidently. "I remember you in diapers. I'm your second cousin, to be exact. I babysat you at Grandpa and Grandma's fiftieth anniversary at the Legion in Stephan."

Family reunions, weddings, anniversaries, funerals snapped like Polaroids. One image came into focus. She saw a redheaded girl in a pink polka-dot dress. "I was wearing a green jumper," Onja blurted, adding, "You're *that* Sara? What are you doing here?"

"I've been cooking at the dig."

"No way…" Onja looked at Etthen. "I'm getting used to surprises."

"Yup, I cook three meals a day for those ravenous archaeologists. I even hear that you sampled my cuisine."

Onja remembered the bag lunch. "Right. It was delicious."

"Okay, knock off the politeness. It was an egg salad sandwich."

They laughed and Onja asked, "How did you know about the dig?"

"Our ranch was just up the valley…our house is still down there, so I'm staying there for the summer with Mom. It's kind of like camping. Dad's found work in the city, so he and my brothers are at our new place on King Street, a few blocks from Grandpa and Grandma."

"Why did you move?"

Sara looked at Etthen. "Is she for real?" she asked. He nodded. She turned back to Onja. "We moved because our land is soon to be six feet under."

Onja replayed the words. Sara didn't seem sarcastic or bitter. "You're saying your house is going to be flooded?"

"Actually, we've sold the house and someone will move it next fall. The outbuildings will be salvaged for wood. Everything else will be bulldozed."

Onja's jaw hung open. She tried to speak but her breath froze. Finally she said, "You don't seem upset."

"It was a little sad at first, but I'm excited about our new place, and we have friends down the street who have an outdoor hot tub. I'll be going to college next year anyway, so what's the big deal?"

Onja sat down in the nearest armchair. How can we be related? she wondered.

Sara continued, "Etthen says you keep a horse. I still have my gelding at the ranch. We should ride sometime."

Onja nodded.

Footsteps clipped on the stairs.

"Hey, Jones," Etthen called. "Sit down for a bit. What's the latest?"

Onja turned to see Jones, cap in hand, standing in the doorway.

"On which front: anti-globalization, poor bashing, greenhouse gas?"

"I want it all, Yoda," Etthen said.

Sara stood. She was at least five feet, ten inches, and all legs. "Can't we just have one peaceful dinner on the town," she said to Jones.

"That's the deal," Jones said. "Will you take a rain check, Etthen?"

"See you later, Cuz," Sara said as she left the room.

Onja listened to their footsteps on the stairs.

"Does he know she's a Claibourn?" Onja said, wide-eyed.

"Sure. Opposites attract."

Onja nodded. She didn't know where to look. They were alone.

"I've been researching your Palliser and Macoun on the Internet," Etthen said. "Do you want to see?"

"Macoun and Palliser?" Onja's investigator's voice was full of surprise.

"My computer is in here. Come on." He led her into Stacy's brother's old room. *I've never been in here before,* she recalled. *Kurt would have killed us.*

Etthen was busy booting up the computer. His clothes were piled in a laundry basket; he had rock and artsy posters on the wall; his tousled bed was in the corner.

One night at camp, some girls were talking about the first times in their boyfriends' bedrooms. Onja's face and throat began to warm. She'd had *that* talk with her mom: boyfriends' bedrooms were definitely off-limits. She stood in the doorway. But *he's not your boyfriend, Onja,* she told herself. *You've got Victor!* She entered the room to examine a poster above his bed.

She jumped when Etthen spoke. "Are you going to stare at the wall all night or come meet Mr. John Macoun?"

She pointed at the poster. "Who is he?"

"Alphonse Sandypoint…a Dene fiddler. He represented northern Saskatchewan at the National Aboriginal Achievement Awards last year in Ottawa." He put his foot on the bed and leaned toward the picture. "See, he autographed it."

Onja moved closer to read the loops and scratches. She kneeled on the bed for a closer look. "Glad to meet a…" she read slowly, then stopped.

Etthen leaned into her shoulder so that he could point at the words as he read. "A promising fiddler…" He hesitated.

"Like you…" Onja read and paused. She could feel his eyes on her face.

"Etthenaze." He finished the sentence, then added, "*Aze*— on the end—means *little*."

"Little Caribou." She turned toward his face. His mesquite brown eyes came closer as his hand left the poster and touched her cheek. She closed her eyes. His breath was as soft as birch bark. His lips brushed once against hers.

Etthen moved backward slowly.

Onja opened her eyes to see him sitting on his hands at the edge of the bed. She sat beside him—not touching— and folded her hands on her knees.

"I should have asked," he said. "I'm sorry." His eyes bore into the wood paneling across the room.

"Etthen," his mother called from the top of the stairs, "can you bring me some ice?"

"Okay," he yelled as he stood. He paused in the doorway and turned around. His voice was quiet and cautious. "Onja, there's a dance in Stephan on Friday. Do you want to go?"

"Uh, yeah…I'd like that." Her voice was almost a whisper.

From Stacy

I don't care if it was a mistake, Onja rationalized. He kissed me, Spaghetti Legs Claibourn. She lay on her bed, hands meshed behind her neck, elbows pointing up. "I'm flying," she told Superman.

Her smile was like a boomerang. She tossed it away. What if I tell him I lied about having a boyfriend? Would he be interested in me? He did kiss me, she reminded herself.

The wide smiling boomerang returned. She could still feel the dusting of his lips, like sugar powder on an éclair, Onja thought, licking her lips.

The evening—after the kiss—had been spent upstairs with the adults. They'd glanced at each other, whispered when they'd passed, yet kept their distance. It had been a dance; nothing like the polka Aunt Rose taught me, Onja thought, or the waltz from gym class. More like line dancing across a chaotic room. Her mother had come at 9:30.

Her smile flew away. What am I going to do now? And what about his girlfriend? His *real* girlfriend.

The boomerang returned, upside-down. I won't tell him I lied. I'll say that I broke up with *Victor* on the phone, this weekend.

Knock…Knock, Knock…Knock…Knock…KNOCK. KNOCK. Her father's familiar "shave-and-a-haircut" signal.

"What?" She flopped her head sideways.

"There's a letter here you might want to see."

"Just shove it under the door."

"As you wish…"

Onja imagined her father bowing. What's with the fancy talk, *as you wish*, she thought. Did he forget he's a farmer?

A *shhhh* delivered a white envelope on the brown and golden carpet. She recognized the handwriting that was less round and more exaggerated than usual: Stacy. Finally!

She flung off the sheet and quilt and dove for the letter. B.B. 1212 Sandsford Road, Medicine Hat, AB. Sandsford Road, Onja thought, sounds a lot more sophisticated than Box 2, Palliser, SK. She slipped her finger between the folds of the glued paper. No. She stopped as though she were about to walk under a ladder. I'll shower first.

She placed the message from her best friend on her dresser, threw her blankets to the floor, then made her bed. She set the white envelope on her fluffed pillow and left the room.

The water rained on her sleepy body and mind. A crystal heart in the window caught and twisted the morning light into dancing rainbows. ROY G. BIV, Onja thought. She squinted as the colors edged her eyes. Red, like rose hips on his tongue. Orange like the taste of his lips. Yellow like candlelight in his eyes. Green like the grass beneath his feet. Blue like the sky against the night of his hair. Indigo like his beating heart. Violet like the warmth of his skin. My goodness, I'm getting good at this mushy business, she thought, smiling to herself.

She toweled off, then snapped her hair forward,

wrapping it into a turban. The mirror caught her bare shoulders and head in a cameo. She pulled a strand of hair from the headdress and fashioned a ringlet. Yes, she thought, he might like me. She leaned toward the mirror. He was this close to me, she remembered. Even closer.

Monday, August 6

Dear Onja,

I received your last two letters on Friday. I would have answered right away, but this weekend was so busy. You know how it is.

I hope this gets to you in time. If not, it'll be a surprise. I'm coming for the Street Dance. Remember the last one, oh yeah, you didn't go…anyway, I'd been telling Cayley and Amber all about it. They really wanted to come, so we talked Mom into driving us, but Cayley had to back out because she's working. But Amber is coming!!! We'll stay with Auntie Moira right in Stephan. Do you think you'll go this time? I can't remember why you didn't before.

Sounds like you're keeping busy stalking your new neighbor. I knew you were desperate, but was it really necessary to injure yourself? Just joking.

I said a good one the other day. I was trying to explain a commercial jingle to Amber. It was a limerick. I said, "Amber, haven't you heard of a *Rimmer—Lick*?"

She said, "You should tell Tim Horton's." I didn't know what she was referring to. So then she had to explain how they had this "Roll up the Rim" advertisement. Get

it? Rimmer for Rim and Lick because it's a donut shop!
Doesn't sound so funny right now, but we killed ourselves
laughing. I guess you had to be there.

Man, your letter is a real novel.

There is one question I can answer. Yes, I've met some
guys. Cayley's older brother is definitely an option.
He's going into grade eleven and just lives down the
street. I see him all the time. He's BEE-U-TEE-FULL.
He swims competitively, so his blond hair is a little
greenish, but he makes up for it in every other way, if
you know what I mean. (I wouldn't have thought you'd
be interested in the boy department, but maybe you're
finally growing up.)

Amber's cousin is pretty hot too. His dad is a rancher.
We went out to their place one weekend and he was the real
thing: dusty cowboy hat, leather chaps, a lasso...wouldn't
mind if he tossed it my way. He cleans up real nice, but I
played it cool. You know, "better shop around." All that to
say, there is no shortage of guys!

Yes, my friends are into fencing. They're both representing
Alberta at the Nationals. They've been after me to join, but I
think I'll just be a groupie. Some of the guys are pretty cute.

See you on the weekend.

Later,

Stacy

Onja put down the letter. She loosened the turban and
rubbed her scalp as if she was trying to erase it.

Under Conscription

Onja was just sitting down to breakfast when Aniedi phoned to request help transcribing her interview with Uncle West. After Onja agreed to help, she reread Stacy's letter, which she'd brought with her to the table. The words were cold and slippery, just like the leftover porridge she swallowed, spoonful after spoonful.

A week ago, I'd have been out of my mind to think that Stacy was coming home, especially coming to the dance, Onja thought. Maybe she's just a horrible letter writer.

Onja let her mind drift to the evening with Etthen, on Ginger, in the rain. She shivered and tossed Stacy's letter into a pile of bills by the phone.

Later that morning, Aniedi laid her laptop on the table in Sylvia's library. Aniedi typed while Onja worked the recorder. Play, pause. Play, rewind. Variations on this pattern kept them busy all morning. She knew that if she told Stacy how she was spending this morning, Stacy would think it was really dull. It wasn't.

They ate hamburger soup from the Crock-Pot for lunch and then wandered into the living room. Aniedi admired Sylvia's camel collection, and she liked the wooden puzzle intarsia clock too.

"I can't believe how long it takes to transcribe something," Aniedi complained. "That half an hour with your dad took me over three hours to type."

"That's six hours of typing to one hour of tape!" Onja said.

"Now you know why I needed you." Aniedi playfully knuckled Onja's head. "I just hope I get quicker at it."

They resumed their stations.

The rhythm of Uncle West's voice sounds like the murmur of the valley, Onja thought, earthy sweet. His voice rolled on. "It was terrible...you could see it come. All of a sudden it was over the dyke."

"Onja." Aunt Hazel's voice was faint on the recording, almost drowned out by the whirring wind. "I want to show you where I kept my garden."

Uncle West continued, "We were able to get the hay off that meadow...but in fifty-three we went up and made the hay at Palliser. They had all that tame government hay...I was in charge of that for two years."

Aniedi typed.

"That's when we started with the VLA."

"The what?"

"Veterans' Land Act. We tore down the other house and built over here. The VLA guy came over and we didn't like his house plan because it was pretty small..."

Aniedi motioned for Onja to rewind the tape. Several minutes passed. Her uncle's voice faded in and out of her thoughts.

"Sure. Of course…things change. It was always tough down here, but after the ditching and draining, people just couldn't make a go of it. The valley wasn't a valley anymore. The river wasn't a river."

"Because it didn't have natural systems?" Aniedi asked on the tape.

"Right. The big problem was no control. When you did get the moisture, you couldn't control it. It was there one moment and gone the next. Nobody had a chance to make any use of it. And then people were draining onto other people. Man, it just about come to blows."

Just about come to blows. Onja replayed her uncle's words. You'd think he, of all people, should see the danger of people rearranging nature. A warmth pulsed in her chest.

"Well, water's so important," Aniedi said. "We take it for granted, turn on a tap."

Uncle West's cough muffled onto the tape. "You got that right. Sure, thousands of acres could be irrigated. But if we don't use the water, the States are going to say, 'Hey, we could use that water.'"

The phone rang.

Aniedi called, "Break time."

Onja paused the tape and walked into the kitchen. "Hello."

"Can you be ready to go in ten minutes?" Etthen's voice was intense, like a police dispatcher's.

"Sure. Go where?"

"Jones is trying to save your pump house."

Oilers Cap Guy, Onja thought.

"I'll tell you more when I get there." He hung up.

Aniedi entered the kitchen, taking a long drink of bottled water.

"I think I'm going somewhere right away," Onja said cryptically.

"Duty calls?" Aniedi guessed.

"Something like that."

"I can finish the rest of this at my place. Do you want to help me pack up?"

As they loaded Aniedi's equipment into the Firefly, Etthen's black Chrysler smoked up the lane.

Jones was in the front seat. "Get in," he barked as he threw open the front door and jumped into the back.

Onja and Aniedi exchanged a sisterly expression. Onja climbed into the front seat. Etthen waved abruptly at Aniedi but did not grin his silly I-see-Aniedi grin. He sped from the lane.

"Okay, what's going on?" Onja smiled tensely.

Etthen looked into the rearview mirror, cuing the captain in the backseat.

Jones' voice was all business. "A buddy of mine told me a crew is going back to the pump house tonight to finish her off. Etthen had told me you were pretty attached to the place…"

Onja kept her neck straight, but her eyes swung toward Etthen.

Jones continued, "And then it hit me. You are the poster girl for the valley. So I phoned my contact in the media, and he called back that they'd send a camera team."

Onja's head snapped back so that she was eye to eye with Jones.

"Are you ready for a standoff?" Jones' voice drilled into Onja's ears like a jackhammer.

Inside a Huddle

The unmarked country junction—two miles from the farm—looked like a big-city intersection. Three small cars, a truck and one white minivan with SKTV scrolled in red and blue on its side idled at the side of the road, but fell into line behind Etthen's Chrysler as they turned south toward Stony Crossing. A billow of dust followed.

You'd never know it rained two days ago, Onja thought, not knowing what else to think as the drama unfolded around her.

The convoy slowed down only slightly when it hit the road allowance trail, and only a little slower as it bounced over the Texas gate.

The odd collection of vehicles twisted its way onto the valley floor to find the pump house matched against the bulldozer, but no other players in sight.

Baggy pants, bandanas and loose T-shirts emerged from the three small cars. Jones ran to meet them. He looked out of place with his Oilers hat, but he pointed and soon back-packs, looking like military gear, lined the ground.

One of the girls pulled a hose and then a mask from one of the bags. "Get a picture of this," she called toward the minivan as she pulled the mask over her mouth and started posing.

The others laughed, and a tall young man yelled, "Bring it on."

Onja, who still sat in the front seat turned to Etthen. "Is this what I think it looks like?"

Etthen overplayed a smile and rubbed his hands like a wicked mastermind, bent on world domination.

"This is Palliser. We don't protest," Onja deadpanned.

"Technically, this is the CPR pump house. And technically, you are now a protester." Etthen leaned over and whispered, "This is all for you."

"I didn't ask for this," she whispered back.

"Yes you did." He reached for the door handle and left the vehicle.

Turning her eyes away from the people, she looked into the face of the pump house. It had been a house, a home. Children had played right in this yard. She had played here. And now *they* were going to push it over so some fishermen could dream to drive their boats where the sky now dwelt.

Coals, which had been smoldering in Onja's chest, licked to life with this breath of fresh-air reality. She opened the door slowly, stepped out and stood beside the vehicle, the coals now flaming.

"Yes, I did ask for this."

Jones waved her over and introduced the group: Angela, the gas-mask poser; Rob, the teaser; Janna, the giggler; Bev, the big-eyed; Debbie, the quiet; Robert, the hummer; Michael, the tall one, and Onja lost track of the others' names.

"Here's the plan," Jones said in a whisper, as though the abandoned valley had ears. Onja, wide-eyed, listened intently to every detail.

A far-off rumbling arrested the small gathering's attention.

Jones released them from the huddle.

The SKTV team of reporter and camerawoman leaned toward one another, speaking quickly, like a skip and third before last rock in a curling game.

A lone half-ton came into view, slowly navigating the valley floor beside the riverbed.

It was as though someone yelled "Action," Onja thought.

The small-car team, as well as Jones and Etthen, circled the pump house, arm in arm, hip-deep in mature grasses, some of them inside the bucket of the orange bulldozer. The tall man, Michael, pulled a sheet of paper from a black portfolio folder and stood on swathed ground near the front door of the pump house.

Onja looked from side to side, like an actor who's forgotten her lines.

Etthen whispered, "Onja, go stand with Michael."

She walked with a determined stride and joined the tall man. Together they faced the approaching truck.

Two older men—one in an orange hard hat, the other in white—swung the truck doors open and stepped onto the packed trail. The expressions on their faces seemed to say, *We see this sort of thing every day.*

They walked directly to Michael. The orange hard hat spoke. "You in charge here?"

"You bet I am," Michael said.

Irony hung in the air like a pair of brand jeans on a hippie clothesline.

"Me and George here have orders to finish up this project. You'll kindly tell your friends to vacate the premises."

Michael flashed a three-piece-suit smile. "My people won't be leaving until our job here is done." He extended the white sheet of paper to Hard Hat. "As you will read on this document, there is insufficient environmental study on this heritage building. Your project here won't wrap up anytime soon."

Without reading the sheet, the two men turned abruptly and walked to their truck. George picked up a phone while Hard Hat skimmed the sheet.

Onja looked up into Michael's face.

"So far, so good," he mouthed, sounding more like a giddy schoolboy than a tough negotiator.

Onja glanced backward. The arm-to-arm ring hugged the pump house, leaving the orange threat outside the circle. Nobody smiled or betrayed any emotion. In her peripheral vision, she could see the camera panning from the truck to the protesters. The reporter now stood in front of the camera, speaking.

A truck door slammed. Hard Hat walked back to Michael and offered the paper.

"Nope," Michael said, "that's your copy. I have plenty more where that came from."

The older man made no reply, folded the paper and tucked it into his denim workshirt pocket. He scanned the scene, like a trained first responder surveys a crisis, then turned and walked quickly to his truck.

The reporter called out, "Sir, do you have any comments? Sir?"

He kept walking.

George, who was still on the phone, made eye contact with Michael as the truck spun in a circle and headed back the way it came.

The pump-house huggers cheered and exchanged high fives and handshakes.

The media pair turned and raced toward Michael and Onja. "Mr. Martin, a few words please?"

"Sure." Michael pretended to straighten a tie that wasn't there. "Just let me freshen up."

"What just happened here?"

"As you know, I'm an environmental lawyer; however, I was happy to copy a little law for our deconstruction friends regarding the guidelines they are obliged to follow when demolishing a property which has been abandoned."

"Where did they go?"

"Likely back to talk with their bosses, who will then talk to their lawyers. I estimate they'll be back in less than an hour."

"And how about you, Miss Claibourn? What do you think about what you've just seen?"

Onja looked up at Michael, who nodded back to the reporter.

"I've heard about things like this…protests. But I've never been in one before." Onja peeked at the pump house. "Up until today, I thought I was the only person who thought this dam was a dumb idea. I guess I don't know what to think. I never realized I could do anything to try to…to save the valley."

On the Six O'Clock News

Horizontal rays of honey light turned the valley into a world of rich golds, greens and browns. The eastern hills, and the river they bordered, disappeared around a bend, while the western hills vanished into the sun. Cumulous clouds drifted closer.

"Did you ever look for cloud shapes when you were younger?" Onja's face lifted to the sky as she spoke to Etthen.

"Sure. Mom has a cloud thing."

"What do you see?"

Etthen did not look skyward. His gaze was on Onja.

"Etthen, it's about…I need to tell you about…Victor." She swallowed. "There is no Victor. There never was a Victor. I don't even know where I came up with that name. Nobody's named Victor!"

"I have a cousin Victor."

Onja laughed. "You're not mad that I…lied?"

"Let me put it this way. Up until yesterday I had two problems. One, I had a girlfriend. Two, you had a Victor. Last night I took care of problem one with a phone call, and now you tell me there's no problem two."

"Hey, you two," Jones interrupted, "don't burn all your energy in one place." He flashed a knowing grin and tossed two chocolate power bars into the air, which Etthen and Onja each caught with a swing of their right hands.

"Hey, yeah, I am getting hungry," Etthen said.

"They're real professionals, hey?" Onja looked to the laughing gaggle of protestors. "Is there anything they didn't think of?"

The grinding of vehicle wheels on gravel sounded like the unwrapping of the foil-covered bars. Onja looked to the trail on which they had entered the valley hours earlier. Mom and Dad's white half-ton.

Etthen followed Onja's eyes.

She almost said, *Now I'm in trouble*, just like a kid in grade four announcing, "My mom's going to kill me," when she shows off her grass stain to her friends. Parents were expected to be angry about things like this.

As the truck grew larger, Onja felt a pulse of peace like the relief she felt after a good cry. It didn't matter what her parents threw at her, because it wasn't about them. It wasn't even about her. It was about the valley.

She bit into the energy bar and chewed slowly.

Sylvia and Wayne stayed in the truck, eyes locked on their daughter. Onja's eyes first examined her mother, then her father.

"Hey, what's in the back of the truck?" Etthen broke the silence.

Wayne opened the half-ton door and walked to the rear of the truck to unlatch the tailgate. With a leap Onja had seen her father make thousands of times, he was in the truck box. He pulled the barbecue to the edge and called, "Anyone want to give me a hand here?"

Etthen bounded forward.

Sylvia jumped out of the truck and lifted a red cooler from the back, then returned Onja's jaw-drop with a wry grin.

Soon the barbecue was set up on the packed trail; a card table held drinks, buns and fixings, and Wayne was slapping hamburgers onto the grill.

"Only one thing missing," Wayne said. "Onja, you and your friends go gather some dry wood by the trees over there?"

Onja tossed the power bar onto the dash in her parents' truck.

When they returned with sticks and snapped logs, Wayne started a fire in the bottom of a sawed-off barrel which had also appeared from the back of the truck.

"Corn roast!" Onja announced.

A whoop, a whistle and sporadic clapping were the perfect accompanying music.

"We saw you on the six o'clock news," Sylvia said to Onja, who threw an unhusked corncob into the flames.

Onja looked around. The reporter and camerawoman had not returned.

"Your dad thought you might be hungry."

Onja looked at her father, who was locked in discussion with Jones.

The sun now threw rays of orange, yellow, pink and purple at the clouds. Charred cornhusks had returned to the ground; chewed cobs had turned into a game of how-far-can-you-throw-yours. The lean and mean protesters now looked more like summer-time picnickers, spread out on blankets, heads on laps, lazy grins.

Etthen sat up and looked east. Onja recognized that look, just like Radar in the reruns of *MASH*. He heard something.

They stood as the sound of a distant vehicle—or was it more than one vehicle?—reached everyone's ears. The team gathered its belongings as though surprise company was walking up the driveway.

When three company trucks—followed by the SKTV minivan and two RCMP cruisers—dipped through the last gully and then drove up to the site, the protesters were ready. This time Onja hadn't looked around for directions.

Sylvia and Wayne stood stiffly beside their truck.

The man under the orange hard hat, with five men in tow, walked toward Michael. "Here's your dotted *i*'s and crossed *t*'s," he said, "from our lawyer to you."

The reporter, with camera rolling, followed a short distance behind. The police stood beside their cruisers.

Michael read the typed page silently.

"We have our orders, sir." Hard Hat sounded apologetic.

Michael looked into the weathered face of the older man and spoke softly. "And we have ours." Michael twisted his neck and yelled, "Plan *B*."

Onja turned and ran with Michael to the pump house to join the human chain.

George, under the white hard hat, was already on top of the bulldozer. It roared alive, shaking those who stood in the bucket.

Etthen's right hand gripped Onja's left forearm like a vise. She clenched in return. Onja and Jones clasped arms on her other side.

"Hang on, but don't fight back," Jones coached Onja.

Onja had a clear view when one of the officers grabbed Angela around the waist while another helped pry her grip from Janna. When they had Angela, Janna grabbed the next arm over, and Angela went limp like a rag doll. They dragged her a few meters away, but as soon as they left her to go for another protester, Angela jumped up and rejoined the line.

The bulldozer chugged and belched but did not move an inch forward or back.

Onja felt arms around her middle squeeze tight.

"Leave her alone," Etthen spat.

"Hold the line," Jones reminded Etthen.

A woman officer peeled Onja's grip from Jones, then swung her hard so that she couldn't reconnect. The officer had Onja loose from Etthen within seconds; Jones and Etthen reconnected the line.

Onja went limp, as she'd seen the others do, and let herself be dragged away, but instead of depositing her in the grass so that she could make a run for it, they took her to the police car and slipped her in as if she was a sack of groceries. The door slammed shut, and she realized there were no handles on the inside.

Onja sat forward on the seat to watch the scene unfold. She hadn't noticed a jeep pull up. Jim, Maureen, Celine and Aniedi piled out and went directly to Hard Hat. Celine was speaking, illustrating her words by pointing to a sheet of paper she held in her hand.

The cruiser door opened, and Etthen fell in. He sat up and joined Onja's gaze. "Go, Mom," he shouted.

Hard Hat, followed by the archaeologists, turned and walked toward the nearest officer. They spoke briefly, and the constable called out a command.

Hard Hat climbed up on the bulldozer, caught George's eye and drew a line across his own throat. The bulldozer coughed and fell silent.

A football field cheer erupted; they'd scored the first touchdown.

In a Dam Rumble

Classic rock blared from the open windows as Etthen guided his black-finned vehicle over the gravel road. Onja combed her hand through her windblown hair. Dust and grit had replaced the silk she'd left the house with. She could taste chaff in her mouth. The Johnstons were already combining. Her father had taken the swather out this afternoon, but he said he'd wait a day or two. His wheat was too tough.

The sun was heavy in the peacock sky, like a beach ball with a slow leak, Onja decided. She turned her head from the trail leading to the valley.

When the officer had come back to the car, she'd slipped into the front seat and begun speaking. "How old are you two? You first, sir?"

"Sixteen."

"And you, miss?"

"Fourteen, fifteen on Monday."

"Ever been in trouble with the law?"

"No," Onja blurted.

Etthen remained silent.

"And you, sir?"

"What do you think?"

"I think you're old enough to speak for yourself."

"Sure. I've thrown an egg or two, back in the day."

Etthen and Onja turned onto the highway toward Stephan. They had been alone in the vehicle for over five minutes and neither one had spoken. Wish I'd worn a black T-shirt rather than this skimpy white thing, Onja growled at herself. She pulled at the short shirt, trying to lengthen it over her flat stomach.

"About yesterday," Etthen began softly and then paused. "We sure gave 'em hell!"

A crooked smirk wriggled on Onja's face. "I've never been so terrified, and had so much fun, all at once."

She folded the *Dam Rumble* brochure in her hand.

"Where do I go first?" Etthen spoke.

Onja straightened the paper. "There's a barbecue at six-thirty, followed by speeches at seven thirty. Display tables are open from four to eight. The dance starts at eight. Jones wants us to infiltrate. Go on a fact-finding-mission."

"We'll make the barbecue with time to spare." He turned the knob on the radio and the music mellowed. "What time are you supposed to be home?"

"Mom said midnight, but Dad said eleven. So I guess it's eleven thirty."

Etthen reached over and squeezed her hand.

"My best friend is supposed to be there tonight." Onja watched the white line on her side of the road.

"The one who moved to Alberta?"

"Yes. Stacy…and she's bringing a friend. Amber."

"Are you excited?"

"Of course," Onja answered. That sounded fake, she thought.

Etthen rested his elbow in the window. Onja greeted each landmark into the small prairie city as if she was seeing it for the first time. The cemetery with plastic flowers at every mound and no granite headstones. The semitrailer weigh station flanked by patrol cars. The mine museum with a pioneer dragline on the lawn and metal artwork: sunflower, grasshopper, high chair, tool collage.

They drove into Stephan on Main Street. At the movie theater there were bales of hay set up as a roadblock. Etthen found a parking spot on the tarred pavement under the sign *Farmer's Market Saturday 8:00-Noon.*

They walked past the credit union on the corner. This end of the street was also barricaded with bales, and there was a stage set up under the traffic lights. Men in baggy jeans and T-shirts walked this way and that carrying rolls of black cord. Three microphone stands waited on the stage.

"Hope there's no rain," Etthen remarked as they strolled into a wide, open space between the stationery store and the travel agency. "Care for a dance?" he added, grabbing Onja's hands and twirling her around in a mock ballroom style.

"I'll put you on my card." Onja laughed. She had always wanted to say that, just like in the days when society women wrote the names of their dancing partners on cards. Her shoulders dropped and her face relaxed. That feels better, she thought. I didn't know I was so tense!

Halfway down the street an apple red railway caboose sat on a wooden flatbed. "They're really going all out," Etthen said as a woman placed a stand-alone sign in front of the caboose: *Buffalo BBQ Here!*

"Mmm, mm. I love buffalo burgers," Etthen added.

"Never tried one," Onja said.

"What?" Etthen overplayed his shock. "Today's the day to try something new."

"Over your dead body."

"That could be arranged." He pinched her side.

She slapped at his hand. "Watch it."

"I am watching *it*."

"Give me a break." Onja walked ahead. Her mouth was curved into a smirk of embarrassment and pride.

"Okay, okay. Sorry. Hey—wait up."

They walked into the roped section. Round tables covered in red-checked cloths dotted the street. Etthen lagged behind, then called, "Onja, look."

She turned to see Etthen with the cloth on his head.

"Can I join the Kaffiyeh club?" he asked.

"Put that back," Onja ordered in her scolding-Leigh voice.

"Yes, Mom," he teased.

Onja scrutinized his face. What's wrong with me? He even looks good with a tablecloth on his head, she mused.

"How did you get that scar?" she asked, her observation softening his face.

"Long story." He grasped either side of the tablecloth and flicked his wrists above the table, like a hotel maitre d' showing off. The checked cloth obeyed and snapped into place.

"I'm in no hurry," Onja said. She walked closer and smoothed the table as gently as if it were still framing his face.

He pushed down tightly on the back of a chair and spoke slowly. "My dad and I were on the ice…running his dogs…" He gazed north, above the tables, streetlights, buildings. "There was an accident. End of story."

Onja stepped toward a hot-tub booth. "You've never talked about your dad."

"Not much to talk about." Etthen ran ahead. "Hey—it's full." He splashed Onja with bubbling water.

"Did you kids bring your swimsuits?" A shirtless man, sporting a classic farmers' tan, stepped from behind a cardboard display.

"Nope—guess we'll have to skinny-dip," Etthen said.

Onja looked away—now intensely interested in the next booth for the government of Saskatchewan.

"Now you'd like that, hey, son?" The hot-tub man laughed and stepped onto the wooden ladder. "If you find your suits, come back for a soak." His body disappeared into the frothy surface, leaving his chubby, smiling face exposed.

Onja picked up a bookmark with the government of Saskatchewan's website address on it and moved on to inspect golf clubs at the next table.

"Check out those boats." Etthen pointed across the street. "That's a V-180 Intrepid. I bet it has all the features:

fiberglass bow liner, sport seating, sundeck, tilt steering. Would I like to take that baby for a spin!"

"On the Little Mouse?" Onja teased. "What would you do at Stony Crossing? Portage?"

Etthen demonstrated a one-man portage, ending in his collapse under an imaginary sports boat.

"My hero," Onja mocked.

As they passed a fifth-wheel recreational vehicle, set up as part of a display, a familiar face caught Onja's eye. "Look, Etthen, there's Aniedi."

Their friend was sitting behind a table, recording equipment set out. A small bristol board sign, folded in half, read *Tell me your valley story.*

"Etthen," Aniedi called. "Come watch my stuff. I have to go to the washroom." She leapt from her chair and hugged Onja. "Way to go last night. You were impressive." Then she ran toward the washrooms.

Many of the stores were having sidewalk sales. Onja gravitated toward the Horse and Rider Tack Shoppe where beige, tan, brown and black saddles rode sawhorses on the sidewalk. She'd been inside this building as many times as she'd been to Stacy's. She lingered, stroked the padded seat of a two-toned leather model.

"It's beautiful. If I had a saddle like this, I'd never ride bareback again."

"I thought you liked being right next to the horse." Etthen had snuck up on her.

"Yeah, I do. You're right." Onja sighed, then added, more for her own ears, "So why do I love saddles so much?"

They wandered past the tack store, and Onja sat on one of the single bales that lined the street.

"Great benches," Etthen said as he straddled the bale beside her.

"A little pokey." Onja pulled at the hollow straw. "I wonder where Stacy is."

"People are just starting to come in." He pointed back to the caboose. "Look, there's a line now."

Onja slapped her hand to her stomach as a pang twisted in her gut. "Are you hungry?" She looked into his face. His hair hung down the front of his shoulders, and she resisted the impulse to reach out and tuck it behind his ears. I should sit on my hands, she thought. I want so badly to touch him. She gulped into a dry throat.

"I can wait for my burger, but I'd like a drink. Can I get you one too?" He gathered his hair and held it with one hand, just as she'd seen his mother do.

His face changes with every hairstyle, Onja thought. Now he looks like an artist. "Sure, just what the doctor ordered," she said.

"You wait here and save us a bale." He reached forward and touched her knee. "I'll be right back."

She watched his tall frame stride away, and part of her flew along beside him as the crowd swallowed him.

Another part of Onja had remained behind at the pump

house. It had taken some convincing by her mother for her to leave last night, after the police and company people had left. She had wanted to stand guard over the pump house, and it looked like they were going to have lots of fun too. The protesters had pitched tents, and Robert had pulled out a guitar. But when the case of beer had come out, Onja knew her parents wouldn't let her stay any longer.

She'd ridden Ginger down that morning, packing in breakfast fruit and muffins, and stayed until early after-noon, listening to the young activists swap stories about their involvement in rallies, sit-ins, marches and demon-strations. Some had even served jail time because of their commitment to their beliefs.

Groups of young guys were now gathering in front of the former SAAN store. Onja recognized a few from Palliser, but the rest must have been from other small towns, or city boys from Stephan. Stacy will be happy any-way, Onja thought.

She looked above the heads of the milling crowd. *Beer Garden* a large sign read.

She studied the other buildings. They're all square, she realized. False fronts. I'd noticed Palliser's old-fashioned faces, but I've always thought of Stephan as a modern industrial town. I wonder when this street was built, she mused. Brick, false brick, stone and wooden paneling covered buildings one and two stories tall. Some had businesses or living quarters upstairs. Wrought iron fences circled the trees lining Main. Onja imagined the street with horses and carts. Not a great leap, she thought.

Delicate hands reached from behind and covered Onja's eyes. "Guess who?" a familiar voice sang.

"Stacy!" Onja jumped off the bale and turned around. "Black hair? A pierced nose! What happened?" She stepped back and saw that her friend's pants were almost falling off her hips and she'd had her belly button pierced.

"Onja!" Stacy mimicked. "I dyed my *nose* and pierced my *hair*."

The girls hugged each other and jumped up and down. A strawberry blond girl stood a little way off. Must be Amber, Onja thought.

"Onja, this is Amber…"

"Hi. I've heard lots about you."

"I've heard about you too," Amber said. She was a tall girl with a warm smile, dressed in jeans and a black cotton T-shirt. Just what I should have worn, Onja remembered. Warmth passed over her chest. I'm glad Stacy's got a good friend, she thought.

"So, what are you doing sitting here all by yourself?" Stacy asked Onja.

She looked over her friend's shoulder. "I'm…just…waiting for someone."

"Someone. Is it *him*?"

"Yes." Onja half-smiled. "He went to get me a drink."

"How romantic!" Stacy gushed. "I'm so happy for you."

"Stacy, it's nothing. Really." I hope she doesn't tease me in front of Etthen, she thought.

"Sure it's nothing…"

Onja caught sight of Etthen carrying two drinks.

Stacy followed Onja's gaze. "Is he coming?"

Onja nodded.

Stacy scanned the crowd. "Is he wearing a Levi jean jacket, black belt with a silver buckle?"

Onja wrinkled her eyebrows at Stacy. "He's got a jean jacket, but I didn't notice a belt buckle."

"If that's him," she whispered, "you were way too modest in your description."

Amber laughed. "I'm with Stacy."

"You didn't tell me he was Native," Stacy scolded. "If you put that boy in buckskin, he'd look like the real thing."

Onja looked at Etthen's broad smile as he swerved amongst the crowd with their drinks held above his head. She said, "He is the real thing."

Stacy regarded Onja's understated comment. "I'm sure he is," she said with a husky, knowing voice.

The three girls stood in a semicircle watching Etthen walk toward them. He's not stupid, girls, Onja thought. As if he doesn't know we're whispering about him.

He stopped opposite Onja. "Here's your drink, *deary*."

Stacy and Amber giggled.

Great, Onja thought. He's playing to them like an audience. After the introductions, Etthen suggested they get in line for buffalo burgers. Onja whined, "It's like eating rabbit. I just can't do it." But the pressure from the other three pushed her into line. At the till, Etthen said, "I'll pick those up," and he paid for all four burgers.

"He's a keeper," Stacy hissed in Onja's ear.

At the table, he sat close to Onja and even put his arm around her chair as he teased the other two girls. He has them eating out of his hands, Onja thought.

"How's the burger, Onja," Stacy asked.

"I'll survive," Onja said.

A loudspeaker announced that there would be a few speeches momentarily.

"Potty parade," Stacy broadcasted. The girls beelined for the washrooms in the building behind the beer garden.

"I'll save our table," Etthen called after them.

"Onja," Stacy squealed only a few steps away from their table, before she lowered her voice, "if it wasn't obvious *Longhair* has a thing for you, I'd be all over him."

Onja looked over her shoulder. I was the one who first said Longhair, she thought. But I don't like the way Stacy says it. Like it's what totally defines him or something.

Etthen had turned his chair backward and had his hand on the back as if on a steering wheel. He waved like a farmer, the one finger-twitch, Sylvia had called it.

The girls continued toward the old SAAN store. Onja laughed nervously to herself. I sound like I'm nickering, she thought. I don't like the way this is going.

Amber opened the glass doors to the rejuvenated building.

"Onja, talk to me…" Stacy pulled her old friend's face into hers so that they were eye to eye. "Have you kissed him?"

"No." Her voice was meek, like someone in the principal's office for the very first time.

"Oh, come on. You have too!" Stacy grabbed her hand. "Look me in the eyes and tell me the truth."

"No. I have not kissed him." Don't blink. Don't flinch. Onja fought to keep her composure. She doesn't need to know that he kissed me; technically, I did not kiss him.

Stacy flung the door open to the women's washroom. She strode to the sink and caught Onja's eye in the mirror. Then she turned to Amber. "Can you believe this girl? Somebody so out of her league has the hots for her, and she has made *zero* effort to get him."

Onja went into a stall. At least she believes me, Onja thought, stinging from the verbal slap.

Stacy continued her rant. "You're playing in the big leagues now, little sister. Better watch out or someone will steal him from beneath your nose. I'd love to show him off in The Hat."

Amber joined Stacy at the mirror and they shared a tube of stop-sign-red lipstick.

As Onja walked toward the sink, Stacy slipped a small package into her hand, "Just a little something. Think of it as an early birthday present."

Onja opened her fist. She was holding a condom.

Etthen was not alone when they returned. Onja recognized her redheaded cousin, Sara. Jones sat at the table with his eyes on the podium.

There were a couple of other guys from the archaeology team who were sizing up Stacy and Amber, but Onja didn't know their names. Etthen changed that.

"Stacy and Amber, this is Earnest…yes, his name really is Earnest." Etthen winked at Stacy. "And this is Doug."

Stacy articulated a sarcastic whisper in Onja's ear. "Four girls and four boys. Perfect planning, Onja."

"Yeah, right," Onja hushed back.

"If we can just make it through these speeches," Etthen proclaimed, "the rest of the night is ours." He held up his red Coke cup. Earnest and Doug toasted him with beer in plastic glasses.

"Onja, here, take a seat." Etthen held the chair for Onja. Earnest and Doug followed suit. Sara and Jones were already seated. Jones looked about as happy as a fish on the shore, Onja thought.

The PA system whistled a warning. Tap. Tap. Tap. "Good evening, ladies and gentlemen and…the rest of you, wherever you fit in." A booming voice filled the street. "Most of you know me, Garnet Valentine, from CSJW radio right here in Stephan, sunshine capital of Canada."

The crowd clapped and someone yelled, "More music, less talk." A ripple of laughter danced over the crowd.

"Yes, yes. Our motto at CSJW is 'More music, less talk.' You've got me there. We won't take too long, but we do need to have a few words before we get to the PAR—TEE."

The crowd, including Onja's table, cheered. Everyone… except Jones.

Etthen stood right behind her. He placed his hand on her shoulder and gently rubbed where his fingers touched her neck. Onja remained rigid. Was this for real, or was he putting on a show?

The mayor, the member of the Legislative Assembly, and the member of Parliament brought greetings from their respective constituencies. They spoke of economic development, opportunity and diversification. Onja heard Jones whisper to Sara, "Buzz words."

The announcer called, "And now a word from West Claibourn and the Little Mouse Basin Development."

Etthen poked her. "Any relation?"

Stacy answered, "That's Onja's Uncle West. Dad says he's one of the big dogs behind the dam."

Jones muttered, "Big dog." Sara shifted in her seat.

And Sara's grandpa, Onja thought.

Stacy leaned toward Etthen. "Onja probably told you his life story—how his name is really Wesley, but in the war he was nicknamed West by Ontario soldiers."

"No, she didn't," Etthen said, eyes forward.

Onja stared at the makeshift platform to the side of the old SAAN store. Don't bother with Stacy, she coached herself at the same time, she's in one of her sarcastic moods. Uncle West is in his trademark cowboy shirt and Stetson, and Aunt Hazel looks like she's dolled up for some square dancing, Onja thought.

West Claibourn placed a black briefcase on the podium before the microphone. "Welcome, everyone, to our second DAM RUMBLE." The crowd clapped. Earnest and Doug whistled. Jones scowled.

West continued, "We're really on our way, folks. Just a few years ago, this was all a dream. We dreamed of bringing water to this godforsaken desert; we dreamed of creating a water industry; we dreamed of taking Mother Nature on…and… we're almost there." Whoops from the crowd punctuated the speech. Some people pounded on the wooden tables.

"The dam is built, the park is planned, and Mother Nature is building a life raft." The people nearest the podium leapt to their feet cheering, clapping, whistling and whooping.

Onja watched Jones. He folded his arms and remained seated. So did Stacy and Amber, but they were giggling and whispering.

Onja sat still, stiffly aware. She breathed deeply. Who's speaking for the valley? What about the valley?

Uncle West waved, stepped down and stood by Aunt Hazel.

Then the radio announcer's booming voice echoed through the microphone again. "Let's get this party going." He pointed to the stage at the far end of the street. A country rock band, heavy on the guitars and drums, blared onto the pavement.

Earnest grabbed Stacy's hand and ran for the street. Doug asked Amber if she wanted to dance.

Etthen looked expectantly at Onja.

"I think I'll sit this one out," Onja said, looking to Sara for support.

Etthen snatched Sara's hand and moved to the middle of the two-stepping crowd.

Jones stood up and paced past Onja, who turned to see where he was going. He was beelining toward Uncle West and Aunt Hazel. Onja sprang from her chair and followed.

Uncle West was shaking someone's hand when Jones pushed in to stand face-to-face with him.

"Don't think you fool all of us," Jones said.

"What's this?" West looked honestly bewildered.

"Not everyone thinks you're a hero. Some of us know how sweet you smell after selling your land off to Wise and his government boys."

"Nothing illegal's been done, son." West smiled as he said "son."

"Maybe not illegal on the books, but some might see it as vote buying. Isn't there a provincial election on the horizon?"

"Now, listen here…" West's smile turned to an angry-jaw expression. "I don't know who you are, or what you *think* you know, but if you want to talk with me anymore, city-boy, you can talk to my lawyer."

"Only problem with that is your lawyer's in on all this."

"Why you…" West lunged at Jones, but before he connected, Onja had jumped in between the hostile pair.

"Uncle West, he's trying to get you going. Just walk away."

"Onja, are you with this…" He pointed a finger at Jones' chest.

"No…not really."

"Miss *Claibourn*, then who are you with?"

West took a threatening step toward Jones. "You leave my young niece out of this."

"Uncle West, I am sort of with him."

West backed up and considered his great-niece. "Well…"

"Well, why do you want to flood the valley? It was your home. It was our people's home."

"Ah, dear, these things are complicated."

"Yes, I am finding it complicated," Onja said. "Jones, here, is the only one standing up for the valley. And my family, who should be protecting the land, is partying at the funeral."

Under the Stars

Onja allowed Etthen to lead her away while Stacy and Amber meandered through the crowd. Her heart felt like it had fallen to her ankles. She and Etthen stood in line for a pop and turned to see Sara's folded arms fly above her head. Jones turned his back to her and left. Sara's arms continued, like she's throwing slow-pitch insults, Onja thought.

Etthen whistled a slow exaggerated note. "Wouldn't want to be in his shoes."

Onja's eyes darted past Etthen. "I'd like to tie his shoes together and then push, but he's still the only hero for the valley."

"That's it…" Etthen's voice was like a talk-show therapist's, "let it all out."

Onja smirked.

A peppy polka—complete with accordion—bounced into the airscape. Onja's redheaded second cousin marched toward them. "Good riddance," she exclaimed flatly and reached for a swig of Onja's drink.

They sipped their pops as the sinking sun transformed the clouds into a purple haze. Harmonic chords promised a slow dance. A young man under a cowboy hat asked Sara to dance.

"Come on, Onja," Etthen coaxed, "take a turn with me." He held her hand and she followed him into the crowd of swaying bodies. "Put your arms around my neck," he said as he wrapped his arms loosely around her waist. They floated through the crowd and Onja turned her head sideways, letting her cheek rest against his chest.

Stacy's early birthday present burned like gossip in Onja's front jean pocket. What's happened to my best friend? she wondered, now more sad than angry. Onja looked up into Etthen's face. He squeezed her a little tighter. With all Stacy's big talk, I wonder if she's ever felt this good. Onja squeezed Etthen back.

The song ended and the audience applauded the band. The lead singer announced, "Give it up for Ricki Blondeau, our very own old-time fiddler." There was light clapping and then the buzz of a violin reel woke up the night.

Etthen turned his head toward the music like a wolf to a howl. He tapped his feet a couple of times, a smile escaping onto his lips. Tapped his feet again. Onja stepped back. What's he doing?

Etthen's arms were crooked at the elbow like he was riding a horse, and his feet were prancing on the spot. Is he tap dancing? Onja's jaw opened slightly. River dancing? What's he doing?

Soon there was a small clapping crowd around Etthen. Onja stepped back into the circle and joined in. A thin elderly gentleman with salt-and-pepper hair and a black moustache danced into the circle with Etthen. They faced each other, Etthen's crooked arms barely swaying while the senior's arms swung loosely at his sides.

The circle grew bigger.

The lead singer called out, while the fiddler continued, "Look, ladies and gentlemen. We've got an old-time jigging duel. Looks like we have some authentic Metis form—and, if I'm not mistaken, Dene jigging…Anyone else out there?"

"Here's for the Irish!" a portly white-haired man called as he danced into the circle. "Thank God the song's halfway done," he yelled as the first drops of sweat beaded on his forehead.

A ring of light detailed the trio. Onja followed the beams. Two were directed from the roofs of the banks at either corner and another cast sidelight from above the bookstore.

The fiddler gave a short pull on his bow, followed by a lingering stroke. The song was over. The crowd erupted.

The band surfed the crowd's energy by playing a quick number. "Let's get out of here." Etthen grabbed Onja's hand and they jogged through the two-stepping mass. A few men reached out and patted Etthen's back as he passed. If they put him on their shoulders, I won't be surprised, Onja thought.

He let her hand drop as they stopped under the awning of the shoe store.

"I didn't know you could dance like that!" Onja stammered. "You were awesome!"

"I couldn't stop myself…did I embarrass you?" He kicked at a loose piece of concrete, then looked into her face.

"No…it was totally cool. I've just never seen anything like that before."

"We jig at all our dances. Guess I kind of forgot where I was." He put his hands in his pockets.

"Don't apologize, Etthen," she said. "Really, you were amazing."

A gust of wind blew an empty beer cup over Onja's foot.

"I need some space," he said, looking around like a wanted man. "Let's go for a walk."

"Sure. Where to?"

"Wherever…"

They turned, music at their backs, and walked toward the farmers' market parking lot. The sky was like the purple heart of a storm cloud. Stars were blinking to life with each step they took. "Do you want to get your jacket?" Etthen asked.

"Good idea," she answered.

They walked to the car for the coat, then by gardens and houses with prim flower beds. At a stone church Etthen reached down and took Onja's hand. She didn't object.

His hand is like a sweater in the fall, she thought as their chartless path led them downhill. A guardrail and benches to the side of the road reminded Onja where they were. In the middle of Stephan there was a fenced habitat for antelope, mule deer, white-tailed deer and the kings of the prairie, buffalo. Her dad used to take her there when she was younger.

She let go of Etthen's hand and ran to the lookout point. "Isn't it beautiful?"

Etthen stood beside her, but didn't reply. Onja could feel his eyes on her. She looked up.

He leaned toward her. Their lips touched and Onja kissed back.

A convertible full of laughing teens drove by. "Get a tee-pee," someone yelled, then honked a horn three times.

"Let's keep walking," Etthen said, scooping up her hand. "You know, where I come from there are no restaurants or movie theaters. Going on a walk like this is considered a date." Onja swallowed. A buffalo calf bleated for its mother.

"Look how small your hand is in mine." Etthen gripped Onja's hand entirely in his.

They walked until their footsteps beat in unison. Did he make that happen? Onja wondered.

They retraced their steps all the way back to the street dance.

At the edge of the dance a dozen picketers marched quietly in a ring. When did they get here? Onja wondered. She didn't recognize any of them. Her friends must still be guarding the pump house. They carried signs: *STOP the DAMN DAM!* and *DUE PROCESS!*

Two men—in their fifties, and twins, Onja thought—handed pamphlets to anyone passing to and from the dance.

A hastily made sign caught Onja's eye: *CLAIBOURN GO HOME*.

Not this Claibourn, Onja thought.

The protester turned the corner. It was Jones.

"There you two are." Earnest ran to the edge of the dance area. "I bought you beer." He handed Etthen a cup and turned to Onja, saying, "Stacy told me not to bother getting one for you. Is that okay?"

Onja didn't nod or shake her head.

Earnest looked back to Etthen. "Everyone's been asking for you. They want you and the other guys to dance again. Drink up. I'll tell the band I found you."

A lone fiddle filled the night air. Soon the crowd was clapping and Onja saw the smile on Etthen's face.

"No thanks, Earnest. I think Onja would like my company here."

"Well, whatever, buddy," Earnest said. He grabbed the plastic cup from Etthen. "Guess you won't be needing this."

"Hey," Etthen yelled in dramatic disbelief.

Earnest turned his back. "Hell of a way to spend your Friday night," he shouted over his shoulder.

Onja turned toward the closest protester brother. "Do you have more paper? I have a sign I'd like to make."

Onja took a thick red marker and in block capitals wrote *SAVE THE VALLEY!* then flipped the sheet and wrote *WHAT ABOUT THE VALLEY?*

Within the Briefcase

Sunday morning dawned hazy, but cool. Onja could hear the birds outside her open window. Sunday. A day of thanksgiving and remembering, Onja thought. A day of new beginnings.

She stretched, recalling yesterday. I've never ridden longer or harder. Aniedi was right; it's all about stories.

Onja dressed in a simple tartan skirt and white T-shirt. She left her Bible and open-toed sandals by the front door on her way up the stairs. Porridge bubbled on the stove. She helped herself, but there was a hunger inside her that even the sticky oatmeal couldn't fill.

A breeze of zesty perfume passed behind her. "Onja," her mother said, "Aunt Hazel called earlier…We're going to their house for Sunday lunch."

A sting of sarcasm attacked. Great, Onja thought, maybe Jones will drive by and egg the windows while we're there.

She pushed the half-eaten cereal away from her.

"Can I pour you a cup of tea, dear?"

"I don't feel like tea."

"Nothing like a good cup of tea…"

"Thanks anyway."

Leigh bounced up the stairs singing, "Onja's got a boyfriend. Onja's got a boyfriend."

"Where did you hear that?" Onja snapped.

"Jordan Adams…her big sister was at the dance, and I know all about you and Etthen."

Onja felt the blood rise to her cheeks, as if it was boiling. "Mom, tell her to *shut up*!"

"Onja, you know I hate that word."

"Well, make her go away then…" Onja left, slipping her sandals on before going outside to wait in the car. I'm not in a pew-sitting mood, she thought as she placed her Bible in the back window.

Onja didn't talk when her mother was the next into the car. What was she supposed to say? *The valley is in danger, and none of you will do anything?* Her father honked the horn as soon as he got into the driver's seat. Leigh skipped down the front path.

Sylvia balanced her ceramic mug over Wayne's lap as he drove down the lane. "Maybe you'll watch the road instead of the fields," she complained.

My parents are so dysfunctional, Onja thought.

Leigh worked on a word search for the twenty-minute trip into town.

They parked the car under an elm tree and filed into church. The greeters at the door are like professional salesmen, Onja judged. All smiles and sunshine.

They sat in their regular pew, behind Auntie Rose and in front of the Tuckers. Ouch, this wooden bench is worse than my saddle, Onja thought as the sermon began.

She flipped through the concordance, an index of verses at the back of her Bible, and noticed the word *valley* was a synonym for the word *ravine*. The first indexed verse was Psalm 23:4. Everyone's heard of the *valley of the shadow of death,* Onja thought.

She looked up the next verse. "Multitudes, multitudes in the valley of decision! For the day of the Lord is near in the valley of decision." Onja pictured the stone wall of the pump house, now alone against the bulldozer. Jones' protesters had been called into action in Regina.

She flipped to the first chapter of Joel. Oh yeah, she thought, this is the grasshopper story and Joel is a prophet. She read verse four. "What the gnawing locust has left, the swarming locust has eaten; and what the swarming locust has left, the creeping locust has eaten; and what the creeping locust has left, the stripping locust has eaten."

Last summer had produced a record crop of grasshoppers across the prairies. If anyone drove more than sixty kilometers per hour on the gravel, the windshield would be plastered with bug juice, Onja remembered. And the smell of barbecued hopper on the radiator was hard to ignore. A television station had sponsored a contest:

Who can collect the most grasshoppers? One woman had thirty-two large garbage bags full, and she won tickets to see Elton John in Saskatoon. *Gross!*

And even Dad, Onja remembered, wanted to cash in. He said he could mix the hoppers into the bales and add protein to the cattle and horse staple. She still wasn't sure if he was serious or not.

Onja closed her Bible; the thin, almost transparent paper brushed against the fresh slivers in her fingers. She looked at her hands. Red ink stained her pink skin.

An elderly gentleman led the closing prayer; then they left for Uncle West's and Aunt Hazel's.

The smell of roasting chicken and baked potatoes met Onja and her family before the door to the house opened. Onja wasn't hungry.

"Come on in. Don't worry about your shoes," Aunt Hazel called.

They took off their shoes anyway.

Kids ran through the living room. "We've got Tony's little ones for the day. They're real rascals," Uncle West said.

After hugs, handshakes and kisses, Onja and Leigh joined their father in the living room with Uncle West while Sylvia helped in the kitchen. A beat-up black leather briefcase sat on the coffee table. Onja recognized it from the street dance.

An oil painting of the old ranch hung behind the chesterfield. A smaller photograph hung above the armchair. "Is that MacLeod Lake?" Onja asked her dad quietly.

"You bet," Uncle West answered. "The very same."

"It's so perfect." Onja straightened her skirt.

Wayne Claibourn and his uncle discussed the condition of local crops while Leigh continued her word search.

Onja stared at the painting and then examined her own ink-stained hands. It's like Uncle West doesn't know I'm a protester, she thought. Jones wouldn't visit his uncle if he disagreed with his politics, would he? She hid a smirk. Yeah, I really want to grow up like Jones.

Lunch was catch-up-on-the-family-tree time followed by saskatoon pie.

Wayne and West were talking about plants. "West, let me take you for a drive to the mine's greenhouse," Wayne said. "They've started some of my sea buckthorn. Sylvia, you and Aunt Hazel should come too." He looked at Onja. "You'll watch the kids for a few minutes?"

"Okay." I have nothing better on my schedule, she thought.

Onja followed her charges into the basement where they flopped in front of the television to watch *Lord of the Rings: The Return of the King*. I've only seen this a thousand times, Onja thought.

She dragged herself upstairs, leaving the children hypnotized in front of the TV. She was alone with the briefcase. The lid flopped open easily. Government letterhead. Water management. Ducks Unlimited. Sask Energy. Sask Power. The Legion.

A yellowing letter written on an old-fashioned type-writer was dated 1959. Mom wasn't even born yet, Onja thought. At the bottom were the signatures: Hazel Claibourn, Secretary Treasurer, and West Claibourn, President of the Little Mouse Water Basin Development.

So, Onja thought, feeling low and heavy with this deepening knowledge. My family's been planning this for decades.

Against the Rock

A horse's whinny blasted through Onja's open window. She jumped out of bed and tripped to the screen.

The radio alarm switched on, playing the last chords of a country song.

Ginger's long muzzle mouthed the tall grass at the edge of the window. She looks like a camel, Onja thought. Ginger bared her teeth and cropped a jawful.

"How did you get out?" Onja squinted into the sunny morning. "Why is your bridle on?"

The mare answered with a nicker.

"That's helpful." Onja pulled on pants and tucked in her nightshirt.

The morning man's voice was deep and playful. "Quite a mystery unfolding this morning in the Little Mouse Valley. If you didn't hear earlier, the valley now has a voice."

"Yes, Garnet, we've had some interesting calls from valley listeners this morning." His co-host, a woman with a raspy voice, jazzed into the conversation. "Signs are popping up all over the Little Mouse flood zone."

Onja sat down on the edge of her bed, a smirk pulling at her lips.

"My favorite so far is the series of three: I am yesterday, I am today, I am tomorrow," Garnet said. "The valley's being a little dramatic, don't you think, Judy?"

"Well, I don't know about that. I think it's about time we heard from the valley herself."

"Herself? Maybe it's himself."

Ginger whinnied.

"Just a minute, girl; I want to hear this."

"Himself? A *himself* could never be that poetic. I am home. I am family. I am here. I am memory. I am listening. I am alive. Nope, the voice of the valley is definitely female."

Ginger snorted.

"Okay, okay," Onja said distractedly.

"Well, Judy, we know the voice of the dam is male. Here's West Claibourn himself, who just phoned in and left this message…"

"When I heard about these signs posted in the valley, Hazel and me took a drive. And damn, if they didn't just about make me cry. Nobody loves that valley like I do. So, my hat's off to the voice of the valley."

Onja felt a buzzing between her temples as if she'd swallowed a bee.

"That's quite something, Garnet. Do you think that West Claibourn is having a change of heart?"

"Not a chance, Judy."

Ginger stomped her hoof.

Onja turned off the radio and went outside in her bare feet. "Ouch, since when do I have wimpy feet?" she complained as she stepped on a stone by the path. "What the…?"

Onja rounded the house and saw her mare under a luxurious padded saddle. Onja glanced from side to side and walked cautiously forward. It was the chocolate and tan saddle from the Horse and Rider Tack Shoppe. A purple and white bow decorated the saddle horn, and a tag fluttered in the breeze. She caught the small, hand-addressed card. *Happy 15th Birthday, Onja! Love, Mom, Dad and Leigh.*

Onja's eyes blinked dryly. She looked around again, then felt the plush seat, the ribbed edge, the solid horn, the wooden stirrups. She stood back. "Ginger, you look like a real horse."

Her mother's laughter reeled from her bedroom window directly above. "Happy birthday! Do you like your gift?"

"Mom…it's…"

There was a crash and rustle in the Manitoba maple grove fifteen feet away. Leigh emerged, followed by Wayne carrying a camera.

"Good one, hey," Leigh called. "I kept it a secret for a whole month. That's a record!"

"Dad…" Onja stopped, her words caught in her throat.

Her father grinned broadly. He walked quickly to the horse and began examining the saddle. "This is top of the line. Look at the quality of this stitching. It'll be an heirloom."

"But Dad," Onja choked, "it's too much."

"Not everything is about money, you know," her dad answered. A crooked Claibourn grin crossed his face.

Onja felt her mother's hand on her shoulder. "Now you can go on one of those trail rides that the Fosters lead."

"Well, get up there," Wayne said. "I want to see what you think." He unlatched the lead from the mare's halter and coiled it around his thumb and elbow.

Onja's bare left foot slipped into the stirrup and she easily mounted the saddle. "It feels like sitting in a theater chair," she blurted.

"There's one more thing," Sylvia promised. "I'll be right back."

"Take a spin," her father encouraged. "Saturday was just the beginning. You've got many more miles to cover."

Onja locked eyes with her father. He knows, she thought. And now he knows that I know that he knows.

Onja kneed Ginger and reined her to the right, walking slowly in a circle in the front yard, feeling a security and balance she'd not experienced in the old black saddle.

Her appeared in the doorway, hands behind her back. Onja brought Ginger closer. "Here's your present from Thomas." Sylvia produced a pepper-red leather cowboy hat.

Ginger lurched and eyed the colored hat.

"Easy, girl." Onja patted the side of the mare's neck.

Sylvia held it up and Onja lowered her head, allowing the hat to hide her bed-head hair. "He got this at the Calgary Stampede. It's the real thing! He wondered if it might fit over your Kaffiyeh."

Onja giggled.

"Wayne, get a picture of that."

"Let me at least get dressed," Onja said, pulling at her nightshirt.

"Nope, one for the records." Wayne snapped.

"Dad," Onja whined.

"Can I have a ride?" Leigh interrupted.

Onja leaned forward and rubbed her horse's shoulder. "We're going to go places, hey, girl." She dismounted and held Ginger's reins for Leigh.

"I'll have a quick shower and then go for a ride. Is that okay?" Onja looked at her parents.

"It's your day, Onja," Leigh advised with ten-year-old wisdom.

"Out of the mouths of babes," Sylvia said.

Onja was all in blue, except for her fiery hat, as she swung into the saddle and let Ginger start down the lane. I don't need to direct you, Onja thought, you know where we're going.

Past the lane and the caraganas, Onja yanked the reins. "Whoa, girl." The valley was hidden behind hills, and the farm was behind the shelterbelt of trees. "It's just you and me." She examined the golden highlights in Ginger's tussle of mane below the saddle horn. The birthday girl removed her new hat and then gazed into the sky long enough for the white light to trigger tears. She sneezed.

Onja stood in the saddle, then dismounted. The gravel squished under horse's and girl's plodding feet. The early sun warmed her, but there was coolness on the wind. Hints of the fall, Onja thought. Her heart ached as it did every autumn when the poplars turned yellow and the maples intensified to orange. I always want to go...just to go anywhere in the fall, Onja thought. She was homesick. A homesickness that strikes before you've left home. Could there be such a thing?

The red willows, from a distance, burned in the sunshine like a grove of pencil crayons labeled Indian paintbrush.

The recent rain freshened the grasses in the ditch. The ripening crops sent pungent whiffs of cereal into the air. Soon I'll be riding the bus into Stephan for school, Onja thought, and winter won't be far behind.

She and Ginger walked together in the season-less, season-full afternoon. Red-winged blackbirds, swallows and magpies swished, mice and gophers scampered and ladybugs and aphids buzzed along, unnoticed, beside them.

Onja opened the gate and began the last leg of the walk toward Soldier Rock. It was a pebble on the horizon that grew into a stone and finally a boulder. Onja climbed the last incline and stood beside the erratic.

The bulldozer still kissed against the pump house.

She dropped Ginger's reins and sank to the ground against the boulder, her hat falling over her eyes.

"Can I join you?" Etthen's soft, familiar voice.

"Any time." Onja tilted her hat back and wiped tears off her cheek.

They sat quietly as the sun claimed the sky. Ginger nickered. Etthen walked toward her. "Fancy saddle. Isn't that the one…"

"Yes. I still can't believe it." She didn't take her eyes off the confrontation below.

"What's this?" Etthen held an envelope in his hands. "It was wedged between the blanket and the saddle. It says, 'To Onja'. Is it your birthday or something?"

"Maybe," Onja said, a faint smile warming her lips.

"I hope it is, because…" He held up a small rectangular package. "I got you something."

She delicately peeled the wrapping paper. A silver bracelet lay on blue pressed velvet.

"Here, let me help you." He lifted the chain and clipped it onto her thin wrist.

Her finger traced the floral pattern on the shiny panel.

"Turn it over," Etthen said.

Onja read, "*Ne-na-sni-ha*." She looked to Etthen and the layer of icy anger melted from her heart. "What does it mean?"

"In our language, we don't have a word for goodbye." Etthen's foot rooted underneath a stem of creeping juniper.

"What do you mean?"

"We don't say goodbye, unless we say it in English."

"What do you do then?"

"We say *nenasni ha*. That means, *I will remember you*."

The tears welled again in her eyes. "I'm such a freak," she said, turning her face from Etthen. *No one would understand.*

"Onja, you're not a freak."

Onja studied his eyes. She sucked in her bottom lip and smiled. She stood, walked toward Ginger and gathered the reins.

"Don't forget this." He handed her the envelope addressed in her mother's handwriting. "And by the way, the red hat's okay, but I still like the Kaffiyeh."

She rode away without saying goodbye, or even *nenasni ha*.

The fieldstone and machine pulled her like the horizon to the setting sun. She rode nearer until she hovered at the edge. A white sign planted in the ground: *I am story*.

A burrowing owl—night and day mixed up—screeched.

High in the saddle, she opened the card from her mother. The cover image was a Western red lily, Saskatchewan's emblem, tall among hillside grasses.

Inside, on a piece of plain, white paper, was a hand-written poem.

A silhouette stretches against the wind—
horse and girl amid waving wheat, flax and barley.
The girl, head covered in a flowing cloth,

drives her horse toward the valley,
and as the Kaffiyeh rustles and whips
against her arms, neck and back,
she dreams of distant pyramids, drifting desert
and the boy king Tutankhamen.

Beneath her a rhythmic lunge and pull—
shoulder, leg, hoof—
as her horse pounds the packed prairie trail.

On the valley wall they stop and stand like sentries—
one moment, two, three—
before picking their quiet way
between buffalo grass, buck brush, leafy spurge, cactus,
rock moss, summer sage, creeping cedar, brome,
and the omnipotent sun watches
from her vista in the sky.

Onja stared at the words until her mother's script began to swim. Then she folded the paper in quarters and returned it to the envelope.

Ginger swung her neck sideways and nudged Onja's foot with her muzzle.

"Yes, it's time to carry on, girl," Onja said, her words barely audible in the warm, mid-August breeze. She adjusted her body in the new saddle as if she'd always known it and lifted her face to the sun.

Author Acknowledgments

Confession time. I never used to read author acknowledgments. Now I get it.

Michael, you have encouraged at every turn and endured my angst. I'll keep trying to be as good to you as you are to me (and I forgive you for falling asleep on page 54). Victoria, you took me seriously before anyone else did. Moira, nobody comforts me the way you do. Arwen, thank you for those long, long naps and all the cuddles in between.

Mom, you read aloud Lord of the Rings in three-hour chunks and taught me housework can wait. Dad, you took us into the pasture to see the spotted fawn that I nearly stepped on. Ian, how much did you donate to my new computer? Andrea, I'm so glad you're cooler than me. Grandma Lavine, you reminded me to remember the coyotes. Grandma Laura, I can still hear your laughter. Grandpa Cecil, you read my story before any of the family. Grandpa Pete, your people gave me the valley. Uncle Jack, you opened the briefcase and let me peek. Aunt Joyce, you opened your heart. Mom Koops, you always believe in me. Aniedi, you insisted we take showers at your house the summer we had no water and you let me steal your beautiful name!

Jim Finnigan and Maureen Rollins, you let me interview you before I had a clue about archaeology in the valley, or a clue about writing, for that matter. Your passion has stayed with me. Roy Sanderson, your dedication to history is inspiring. I look forward to learning much more from you. Verna Gallen, your generosity is legendary in my writing pursuits. Thank you for the dialogue! Tim Jones, of the Saskatchewan Archaeological Society, thanks for lending your expertise.

Lisa, you said, "I'm going to write a book some day" and planted the seed. Karen, you let me read my writing to you if I'd scratch your back at the same time. Janna, you read some of my earliest novel scribbling. Ange, you said "Uh-huh" until I talked you to sleep. Rob, you started writing songs. Jodine, you read my first draft with the same care you held my six-week old Moira. Lowell, I hope I didn't use too many big words (had to be said). Joyce, you laughed rather than cried when I said, "Heshte la coffee." Ann, you were first my interpreter and then my friend. Deanna, put down the ruler and step away from the desk. You said it first!

Thank you to the volunteers and staff at the Saskatchewan Writers Guild, the Sage Hill Writing Experience, and the SWG's Mentorship Program.

Kit Pearson, you told me not to quit my day job, but then read chapter six to the group. martha attema, your friendship taught me that it's okay to be passionate about my words. Cathy Beveridge, you braved two Sage Hill Experiences with me, and you gave me Offside when I desperately needed it. Jo Bannatyne-Cugnet, you said, "What's a girl from Macoun doing here?" and you understand the Little Mouse code. Norma Charles, you didn't throw things at the paper-thin wall when you heard me playing my guitar. Kathy Cook Waldron , your feedback was first your smile.

Kevin Major, you sang a song with me for every province in Canada. Curtis Parkinson, you said, "I like the ending, Sheena," when I was ready to throw in the towel. Diane Salmon, your laughter and love for your family reminded me to relax. Art Slade, you told me, "Remember, this is supposed to be fun." Joan Weir, we went to church together and sang late into the night. Amy Nelson-Mile, you made me feel like a grown-up writer, right from the start. And Steven Ross Smith, keep fluttering!

Shelley A. Leedahl, you breezed into my life with the words "Stop stressing…I'll watch the side of the road for deer." We went from zero-to-sixty in four mentorship months (and no animals were harmed during the writing of this novel). Your patient instruction and love for prairie images made all the difference.

Thank you also to Alison Lohans for your generous friendship and for bringing Anne, Donna, Gail, June, Marie, Nanci, Paula and Terry into my writing world.

Sandra Davis and Sharon Hamilton, your camaraderie keeps me going. Here's to many more shared victories, with you in the lead!

Thank you to my students and colleagues at Luther College High School, Father Porte Memorial Dene School, Wolseley High School and Bert Fox Community High School. You were my first writing community. And to the Scenic Valley, Qu'Appelle Valley and now Prairie Valley School Division, thanks for helping me find my voice as a valley girl.

Thank you also to my professors, Dr. Wanda Hurren, Dr. Meredith Cherland, Valerie Mulholland and Dr. Carol Schick, whose questions help me question. I have a lifetime of learning ahead.

Bob Tyrrell, my publisher and editor, thank you for your generous encouragement, subtle insight and empowering vision. Next to horses, orcas are my favorite animals. Now I know why!

And to the Creator of the valley and the Author of my life, I give thanks.

Voice of the Valley is Sheena Koops' first novel. She is an author who has stuck to the old adage "write what you know" and that faith has served her tremendously well in this compelling story. Sheena Koops teaches high school and lives with her family in the historic Qu'Appelle Valley in southern Saskatchewan.

www.sheenakoops.com